Tiger Beetle at Kendallwood

Classic Collection #2

Norma Jean Lutz

NUWS Link, Inc. Publishing

Contents

Dedication

This book is dedicated to:

William, Rhonda,

Elisabeth Nichole, Matthew Alexander, and Ethan Zane Huber.

My love for you exceeds all the words I have ever written!

Preface

AUTHOR'S NOTE

A note from the author:

I love to hear from my readers. You may contact me here:

https://www.normajeanlutz.com

NormaJean@BeANovelist.com

http://www.beanovelist.com

https://www.cleanteenreads.net

Tiger Beetle Photo:

Dr. Hays Cummins

Director, the Inquiry Center

Professor, Western & Geography

Miami University

Oxford, Ohio

Introduction

A Word about the Norma Jean Lutz Classic Collection

During my writing career I have been privileged to have over 50 titles published under my name. Due to the nature of the publishing world in days past, most of these titles were off the shelves and out of print in a short period of time. Sad but true.

Now, a new day has dawned in the word of publishing. Digital publishing and independent publishing have created the opportunity for my past titles to be reintroduced to a whole new generation of readers.

These stories are timeless in spite of the fact they were penned several decades ago. Hence, I have chosen to call them the *Norma Jean Lutz Classic Collection*.

Tiger Beetle at Kendallwood is Book #2 in the Classic Collection series.

I'm excited to be able to bring these stories out of the files and into your hands. I hope you enjoy your read.

Chapter One

Marcy Hankins was carefully skimming the pond with her long-handled dip net when she first heard the sound of motors. It startled her so that she lost the water strider that had been gracefully gliding toward her on the placid water.

It was impossible to think anyone would be driving up the sweeping curved driveway to the deserted Kendallwood estate. No one had lived in the Victorian-styled home for many years. Although empty, it had consistently been kept in good repair and stood as a proud sentinel over the spacious grounds.

Even Bitsy, the mahogany-colored dachshund, lying fat and lazy in the grass nearby, heard the sound. The dog's deep-throated little growl convinced Marcy that it hadn't been her imagination. She arose from where she'd been poised near the water's edge and moved noiselessly to lightly touch Bitsy's head. The touch was comforting, as Marcy's heart had unexplainably sped up its beating.

"Easy, girl," she said softly, "probably someone turning around in the drive. You know how people get turned around in these hills."

Although she'd planned to stay on the grounds for another hour, Marcy lay down her dip net then methodically gathered her belongings, placing them neatly in her blue backpack. She stopped again. It was the sound of yet another vehicle which revved up the drive and cut to a stop.

Bitsy cocked her head as her perceptive ears caught the vibrations of voices coming across the shimmering summer air toward them.

Hurrying now, Marcy grabbed the kill jar in stuffed it into the backpack with her other things. Only a few good specimens were in the jar, but now she must leave. No telling what was going on out front. Perhaps it was thieves, or someone meaning to do harm to the place.

The estate was now owned by a great grand-niece of the original owner, Jason Kendallwood, but no one had ever seen her as far as Marcy knew. Instead, the niece paid Mr. Walsh, the high school custodian, to come out and keep up the place.

Marcy brightened then. It could be Mr. Walsh's pickup she'd heard pull in. Although she couldn't imagine him getting out in the heat of an Oklahoma August afternoon. And she distinctly heard *two* vehicles come to a stop.

The Ambrose County Fair was less than a month away and Marcy planned to enter a complete display of aquatic insects as her 4-H project. But she wasn't making much progress. Even her general display case left much to be desire. She'd hoped to capture a six-spotted tiger beetle soon. She'd even seen one recently with its bright metallic green body scurrying quickly through the grass, but it proved too wily for her. This interruption could hamper her work on finishing the cases on time.

She twisted around to lift the backpack up and slip her arms into the shoulder straps. In her hands she carried the dip net, and also the sweep net used for butterflies and other flying insects which gathered and in the tall grass and wildflowers surrounding the pond.

The sloping expanse of land behind the Kendallwood house at one time boasted luxurious gardens, or so Marcy had heard. It wasn't difficult for her vivid imagination to envision formal walkways, precisely trimmed shrubs and immaculate floral displays being enjoyed by elegantly dressed ladies led about the gardens on the arm of handsome escorts.

As she made her way up the shallow natural stone steps toward the back of the house, there came the sound of harsh grinding of gears which could only be made by a truck—a large truck at that. Now Marcy's heart was thudding and there came a tightness in her throat.

If all this commotion belonged to people who had a right to be here, it might be very uncomfortable to explain her presence on the property. And if they were intruders, she didn't want to be seen at all.

Off to the west of the house, between her and the road were several acres of trees, replete with thick underbrush. In a moment's decision, she left the stone steps and took off across the yard and opted for the trees—far enough away to see, yet not be seen. Actually, it was a shortcut to the winding road in front of the Kendallwood estates, but inconvenient because of the tangle of low-growing weeds and brush.

Parallel with the front of the house now, Marcy could see the driveway through the thick trees. One of the vehicles was a bright orange moving van.

"Oh Bitsy, no," she gasped under her breath. "It can't be. They'll ruin my research projects." She felt her eyes burning with hot tears. "Someone's moving into my little haven."

Her intentions to cross over to the road and leave for home were forgotten. She leaned the nets against a tree and slipped out of her backpack.

"Quiet now, Bitsy," she whispered, lifting the small dog into her arms to keep her from barking. "Let's take a look."

Nervously, she moved through the unwieldy brush, stroking Bitsy's silken ear. Her mind wrestled with the fact that someone was actually taking over the place where she'd enjoyed such wonderful privacy these past few months.

Presently, she was standing directly behind the privet hedge bordering the drive. A breeze, which ruffled her short hair, felt cool against her perspiring forehead. She swiped damp strands from her face with the back of her hand and peered through the tracery of green to view the scene. The moving van was backed up to the portico fronting the large double doors at the entrance of the house. Some distance away was parked a late model station wagon and behind it sat a delightful Corvette painted candy-apple red.

Muscular movers were at work bustling in and out with their cargoes. Presently, an elderly man and lady stepped out the front door. The gentleman, appearing well dressed and rather distinguished with graying hair and trim mustache, addressed a worker.

"Can you tell us of a restaurant nearby? It's been a while since breakfast."

"Back down the road near Beltonville is Clyde's Steakhouse. Great place. Best homemade pies in the county." The worker indicated the direction with a jerk of his head as he maneuvered a large box toward the door.

"Thanks so much." The lady spoke in a soft, kind voice. "We'll try to get back as quickly as possible. How long do you think it will take to unload?"

"Greased lightning, lady," said another worker who walked up behind her carrying one end of a stunning brocade couch of emerald green. "We move like greased lightning." The remark caused a twitter of laughter among the men.

At that moment another person came through the ornate double doors, nearly colliding with the couch. A young man—tall, broad-shoulders—whose laugh rang out as he sprinted sideways out of the path of the oncoming furniture.

"Whoa! You nearly got me there!" he said. His pale blond hair shone in the summer sunshine, and from Marcy's vantage point she could see that his face was graced by a set of deep dimples.

Although she was embarrassed to be eavesdropping, she felt almost smug to be viewing the newcomers without being detected.

"Spence," the older man said, "hop in the station wagon with us. We certainly can't all fit into that cracker box of yours."

"Cracker box?" the boy named Spence (she now knew) gave a mocked pained expression. "You hear that, Aunt Daisy?" He turned to the lady, but she was keeping a close eye on how her couch was being taken care of.

"What?" she asked. "Oh sure. Anyplace is fine with me, just as long as we get something soon. I'm starved."

Once again, Spence's hearty laugh rang out. "We're talking about transportation, Aunt Daisy. We're taking the station wagon."

Now the aunt laughed as well. "Oh, I'm sorry, Spence. It's just that I've never watched my brocade couch being transported before. It's nerve wracking. The station wagon's fine. But let's hurry so I can get back and superintend this job."

News in Marcy's home town of Andonburg spread like wildfire. So why had she not been told that someone planned to buy the Kendallwood estate? Resentment slowly smoldered as she regarded these intruders who were spoiling all her plans for the grand championship in entomology at the county fair. No other spot in the area was so perfect and as accessible as the deserted grounds around the estate.

It had been old Mr. Walsh who first suggested she come to the estate to collect insects. She'd been waiting customers in her father's drugstore, scrubbing the malt machine, when Mr. Walsh described to her the profusion of butterflies there. "Looks like it'd be a right good place for you to find those bugs you been a-needing."

Marcy forgot about her work as she had listened to him describe the grounds. "Do you really think I could, Mr. Walsh? I mean, you don't think the owners would mind?"

The old man rubbed the gray stubble on his chin and peered at her through squinty eyes. "I don't see how it'd hurt a thing. Nobody's been around it but me for a long time now."

It was all the encouragement she'd needed. After several months, the trysting spot had grown to mean a great deal to her. More than just a place to secure needed insects. It became a sanctuary of solitude where she could dream and think out her problems without the intrusion of her twin, Cissy, and her younger brother, Bernie.

"Now my special place is being overtaken," she whispered to the struggling Bitsy in her arms.

If only she'd had the good sense at that moment to turn and leave, the most embarrassing moment of her life might never have happened. But she clamped her arms tighter around the dog, who wriggled all the more against her grip, then broke loose and slipped through the hedge, bounding toward the strangers with all the fierceness of a trained watchdog.

"Bitsy! No!" she called to the wayward pooch without so much as a thought for herself. "Come back, Bitsy! Come here now!"

Bitsy, however, was fully convinced she was the only source of protection for Marcy against these strangers, and gave no heed to the calls. She bounded within a few feet of the trio as though to keep them at bay with her chain of piercing yaps.

Chapter Two

Marcy was forced to run down the length of the privet hedge before finding an opening large enough to push through. As she did, she heard a ripping sound and felt her Levis catch in the shrubbery. But now she was thinking only of grabbing Bitsy before she took a bite of someone in her over-excitement of being guard-dog-for-a-day.

The newcomers were startled at first, but as they realized their assailant was quite harmless, they were amused.

"Bitsy, you come back to me this instant!" Now she was thoroughly irritated. The heat of the day was too intense to be chasing after a disobedient showoff dog. Actually, Bitsy belonged to Bernie, but she didn't obey him either.

The young man named Spence advanced slowly toward the yipping dog, speaking in soft tones as Marcy approached. "Hiya, girl. That's a good dog. Just settle down now. No one's going to hurt you."

Bitsy paused a moment, cocking her head to listen to this new voice. In the split moment that Spence and Marcy both grabbed at Bitsy, the dachshund darted aside on quick stubby legs causing the two of them to land in a heap in the graveled drive.

The humiliation was almost more than Marcy could bear. Her face, already sweaty from the heat of the day now burned with embarrassment. Spence was on his feet within seconds, giving her a hand up. After catching her balance, she put a hand to her hair knowing she must look a fright – sweaty, dirty, mussed hair and torn Levis.

Spence laughed lightly as he brushed white gravel dust from his navy cords. "If word of that tackle ever gets back to my old coach," he said, "I'll never live it down. You pack a wallop for a pint-size."

"I'm so sorry," she muttered, looking away and seeing that the moving men also were laughing at the sight. "Bitsy doesn't usually run away."

"No need to apologize to me," Spence said, now with a look of concern. "I hope you weren't hurt." He touched her arm.

Unnerved by the entire incident, Marcy stepped back and assured him with a nervous laugh that she was fine.

"I'm Spence Caldwell," he said, dimples deepening. "And this is my Aunt Daisy and Uncle Fred Vandyne."

They extended pleasant greetings, but their eyes were questioning. "You live around here?" Fred asked.

"In Andonburg." The renegade dog now stood passively at her feet, dripping saliva from her pink tongue onto Marcy's blue tennis shoes. "My father owns Hankins Pharmacy and Drug Store there." She said that hoping to give herself a bit of credibility and prevent their thinking she was a mental case. "I'm Marcy Hankins."

"What were you doing out there?" Daisy asked, not impolitely.

"I... Well, I like to go for long walks and Bitsy here darted away through the trees. She's never run off like that before. Usually stays right with me. Don't you girl?" To which Bitsy gave a little yip as if to substantiate the fact.

As he opened the door to the station wagon, Fred asked, "Can we take you home? We were just leaving to go to Beltonville, but it'd be no trouble at all to take you into Andonburg first."

Marcy's mind flew to her equipment left back in the trees. "No thanks. I enjoy walking."

"You sure?" Spence said. "We're in no hurry."

"I'm sure. But thanks anyway. I'm sorry for the rude intrusion."

"Think nothing of it." Spence laughed again and rubbed his lower back in mock pain. "I'm sure there'll be no permanent impairment."

Had Cissy been there at that moment, her twin would have had answered with rejoining laughter and a lightning-quick comeback. Any adeptness Marcy had at making small talk had long since drained out of her. "Well, bye now," was all she could think to say. She hurried down the long driveway with Bitsy trotting smugly at her heels.

It wasn't until after the station wagon had pulled out of the drive heading in the opposite direction that she slipped back through the trees to retrieve her nets and backpack.

Just last evening her three-minute-younger, but taller, sister accused her of spending too much time in her workroom behind the drug store. "You're going to rot in there with all those yucky bugs," Cissy had declared. "No guy in his right mind would ever want to date a girl who plays around with those creepy things. It's abnormal. Because of you, some of the guys at school even wonder about *me*." Cissy's voice raised in pitch and volume with each word. "If you had a passing interest in bugs it wouldn't be so bad. But no. You have to shut yourself up in that stuffy room and spend hours up at that spooky mansion on the hill every spare minute. It's positively morbid."

It was true she'd never been as socially active as her sister, but she never minded, loving her work as she did. Cissy dated some, but Marcy saw most of the boys in their small high school as boring. Plus, she'd known all of them since they'd been in kindergarten together.

One thing was sure, this Spence character was extremely personable and good looking, and for the first time she was somewhat ashamed of her first love— her fascination with insects.

Back on the road again, she quickened her steps. The narrow, paved road was tree-shaded in these hills that bordered on the Oklahoma—Arkansas state line. It was true what she'd told them about loving to walk. She loved the countryside where the oak, maple, and pine trees grew in thick profusion. She hummed a little tune as she walked along as she thought of the exciting news she had to tell her sister.

For once, Marcy the *bug brain* would be the first one with the news. Cissy, known as the town chronicler, would be the *second* to know. It was almost disgusting how her sister flitted about Andonburg soaking up information at every turn.

By the time Marcy reached the last ridge overlooking Andonburg's four-block main street, she was hot and out of breath. Once on her own tree-lined street, she could see Cissy and their friend, Winnie Denton, sitting on the front porch steps of the Hankin's modest white frame house.

Winnie's high-pitched giggle floated toward Marcy as she approached. Shouts and laughter sounded from a nearby yard where neighborhood kids had congregated—probably for a game of sandlot baseball.

"Bitsy! You're back!" Bernie came running toward her, excited to have his dog back. He was on his knees hugging the dog who was wriggling in appreciation of the attention. "Did Marcy take good care of you? Huh? Did she?"

I took better care of you than you did of me, Marcy shot the silent accusation as boy and dog ran off down the street.

"Hi, you two," she called out to Cissy and Winnie. "Hey, you'll never guess what!" Stepping past the pair, she slung her backpack down on the porch, then propped her nets against the side of the house. "A family is moving into the Kendallwood estate. Can you believe that? After all these years. I saw an older man and woman, and a teen-aged boy who called them aunt and uncle."

"Spence Caldwell!" Cissy leaped to her feet, sending the fashion catalog she'd been reading spinning into the air. "He's finally here!" Grabbing Winnie's arm, she squealed, "Winnie, did you hear that? He's here. Spence is here. Oh, Marcy, sit down quick. We want to hear every teensy-weensy detail of what he looks like. Did you hear him talk? What did he say? I'm dying to know."

3

Chapter Three

Marcy moved to the porch swing and sat down. She had to be imagining this. It was impossible. "You knew someone was moving to Kendallwood and you didn't tell me?" she asked. How could Cissy have known Spence's name?

Cissy picked up the catalog and stepped lightly about the porch in a ridiculous little skip-hop dance. Her hair, a sandy color like Marcy's but longer, was caught up in a pony tail that bounced along with her dance.

"Oh Marcy, this is so exciting. We didn't know until today that he was some relative of the Kendallwoods, but we've known Spence Caldwell was coming to Andonburg for a couple of weeks now. We learned that much from reading the sports page. The fact that he's a Kendallwood descendent is just icing on the cake."

"Sports page?" Marcy wondered if she were being teased again. At times, Winnie and Cissy enjoyed rubbing it in that they knew more about the latest movie stars and singing sensations who thrilled them.

Cissy sent a knowing smile to Winnie who was still sitting on the steps, her arms clasped around her knees. "Marcy, you never listen when we talk about boys," Cissy said as though she were talking to a three-year-old. "If you weren't such a bug brain, you'd have remembered what we said about Spence."

Winnie nodded in agreement. "Don't you remember how excited we were the day we read that Spence was coming here for his senior year? We could hardly believe it. An All-State Football Champion from Oklahoma City coming to our little out-of-the-way town." The pink in Winnie's cheeks nearly matched the red in her hair. Seeing Winnie's ivory complexion turn crimson usually amused Marcy, but now she wasn't amused at all.

Somewhere back in a vague memory, she did recall the two of them going all gaga over some football player. But they were always mooning over someone or other; she'd learned to turn a deaf ear. This was the first time she wished she'd listened.

"We still don't know why he's coming here to live with his relatives, but who really cares why?" Cissy had settled herself now and leaned her back against the clapboard siding of the porch near Marcy's nets and gazed off into space. "Just to know that dreamboat is here in Andonburg is enough. I can see it all now." She gave a melodramatic sweep of her hand. "Spence Caldwell takes our lame football team up out of the cellar and on to becoming district champions. Maybe even state. We'll be famous. Won't it be fabulously wonderfully thrilling?"

But why Kendallwood? Marcy's thoughts continued to tumble over the fact that her place was being threatened. Of course, she knew it wasn't really hers, but she'd grown so attached to it. Now she felt cheated and cut off. Why hadn't Mr. Walsh warned her? Surely he knew what was going on. If she had known, she would never have stepped foot on the place to begin with.

"Isn't it just such a powerful coincidence," Cissy went on, "that Spence's Aunt Daisy Vandyne just happens to be the great grand-niece of the late Jason Kendallwood? That choice tidbit of information I picked up just today." Pride swelled up in her voice. "I heard that Mrs. Vandyne decided, because of her husband's poor health, to come here and refurbish the rundown old dump. Can you imagine that? What a job!"

Marcy cringed as her sister's description. Secretly, she'd toyed with the idea of one day fixing up the old house herself. Many times, she'd peered into the windows to see the room arrangements and to marvel at the ornate woodwork.

"But," Cissy added, "by the time I found out that news, you'd already left to go up there and we couldn't very well come to warn you. Wouldn't that have looked silly for the three of us to be traipsing about when the Vandynes arrived? Can't say I wasn't tempted though. Just to catch one glimpse of our new star player."

Winnie laughed her silly giggle. "We could have told them we were spies from Beltonville football team."

"Oh, Winnie." Cissy's laughter joined Winnie's. "But Marcy, you still haven't told us what he looks like. You said you *saw* them moving in."

"Yeah, tell us everything." Winnie leaned forward so as not to miss one word.

Now Marcy wished she'd never said anything at all. Where could her nosy sister have retrieved all this information? Probably the newspaper office, or the barber shop. She's been known to snatch pharmacy deliveries out of Bernie's hands just to have a legitimate excuse to visit either place. Cissy could pry information out of anyone. But now Marcy was determined she would not be one of Cissy's sources.

She had no stomach to hear any more of their swooning. No doubt later on they'd learn about her ridiculous stumbling in the driveway. They might even be miffed at her for withholding information, but she'd cross that bridge when she came to it. She stood up and picked up her things to go in.

"They were just leaving as I came through the trees," she told them. "I just got a quick glimpse of the guy." That was almost true, she assured herself. "He's big and blond. But if he's such a hotsy-totsy champion player like you say, you knew that much from his picture in the papers."

"Pictures are never as good as real life," Winnie said, wrinkling her freckled nose. "Just tell us what you saw."

"I saw a man and a woman getting in a station wagon, and a big blond dude in the car with them. And there was a red Corvette parked nearby." She reached for the handle on the screen door.

"Just a minute." Cissy spun around on her bottom and put her foot against the door. "You said before that he called the aunt and uncle. You must have been close enough to hear them talking."

"I heard them say they were going somewhere to eat. That's *all* I know." She pulled the screen door hard against Cissy's foot making her yelp. Nimbly she maneuvered her nets in through the door. As the screen slammed, she heard Cissy say, "A least we know he's got a Corvette."

To which Winnie replied, "And that it's red."

4

Chapter Four

After supper Marcy walked from the house to the drug store to mount the specimens she'd collected that afternoon. While her catch had been limited it was best not to waste any at this point, being so close to fair time. The evening was still and warm, with barely a leaf moving on the topmost branches of the sprawling oaks which canopied the sidewalk.

She turned left at the corner that joined to the main street of Andonburg. The red and blue neon sign outlining the words "Hankin's Pharmacy and Drug" had just come on with a fuzzy glow in the apricot-tinted dusk.

Marcy's key made a firm click as she let herself into the dimly-lit store, turning the deadbolt after her and juggling the items in her hands from one arm to the other in the process.

She never bothered to turn on the front light when she came back to work at night. Not that anyone would be fooled into thinking the store was open. No one in their right mind would think a store in Andonburg would be open after six on a weeknight.

The *new* smells of the store came at her in a rush. Soaps, scented candles, food, and medicinal smells all mingled together to form in her mind the memories of a lifetime.

She maneuvered her way around the glass-top tables and wrought iron chairs scattered around the malt shop area where the high school kids loved to hang out on Friday and Saturday nights. The bold colors of lime green, highlighted with bright yellows and oranges had been her mother's idea. The malt shop side of the store was added the year her father purchased the space next door when a barber shop went out of business. That purchase doubled their floor space.

That same year, her father agreed to give over part of the backroom warehouse space to build Marcy a workroom for her entomology work. Marcy knew his decision was more out of self defense than anything else. The table in the corner of the room she and Cissy shared at home wasn't working at all. Concentrating on her work was nearly impossible in the midst of Cissy's incessant griping.

"I can't sleep," she complained to their parents. "When I try to sleep I have nightmares that those creepy crawling things are alive and attacking me."

The clincher came when Marcy wouldn't let Cissy kill a cockroach she saw in the kitchen.

"Wait! I've got to have that cockroach," Marcy declared. "Let me get my kill jar."

"Wait? Over my dead body will I wait," she wailed as she waved a shoe over her head ready to attack.

"That can be arranged," Marcy shouted back.

As she grabbed her kill jar, she heard the slam of the shoe coming down – finishing off the potential specimen.

That evening a family council meeting took place in the Hankin's living room where it was decided that Marcy's work should be moved to the back room of the store to keep peace in the family. At first, she'd felt like an exile, but as time passed, she grew to enjoy her secluded nook almost as much as she enjoyed being at Kendallwood.

The long table that lined one wall was strewn about with spreading boards, pinning blocks, and long insect pins. With quick efficient movements she made order of the mess and set about to mount the ones she'd collected that day, adding them to her ever-growing display case.

As she worked her inner hopes alternately rose and fell as she looked through the aquatic insects gathered that afternoon, plus a few beetles. In the final analysis, there hadn't been as many nice ones as she'd hoped. Nor had there been much variety.

Various jars nearest the window contained larvae being reared under her watchful observation. From a small refrigerator in the corner of the room, she brought out lettuce and milkweed leaves. Monarch butterfly larvae, she knew, had an appetite for milkweed. As she worked with each jar, she jotted notes of progress in a log book kept close at hand. The monarch would be forming its chrysalis soon. It would bear close watching in the next week or so.

A larva spinning a cocoon or forming its chrysalis was one of the miracles that infatuated her about the insect world. How could a mere worm change so completely and emerge so beautifully as the regal monarch or the downy cecropia moth whose wrinkled wings unfolded until they were five or six inches across? And how could anyone refer to such beauty as *yucky bugs*?

It required immense patience in order to rear insects, which resulted in the fine specimens in her display cases. Moths and butterflies raised under controlled conditions have wings that are virtually flawless.

Nearly finished with her work, Marcy once again studied the cases. Her collection was okay, but certainly not her best. Her toughest competitor at the Ambrose County Fair would be Wesley Pennington, who had consistently won out over her for years. She had dared to think at the beginning of the summer that this might be the year she that she would take the Grand Champion award right out from under his nose.

Wesley, an upcoming senior at Beltonville High, belonged to a strong, active 4-H club there. The Andonburg club was weak in comparison. If it were not the base for her entomology work, she wasn't sure she'd be a member at all. Mrs. O'Bannon, the present leader, was a rather flighty type of lady who had a finger in every pie in town. And her two noisy disobedient little boys had a way of spoiling every meeting. Cissy had dropped out of 4-H work a year ago, having become bored with it all.

As Marcy closed the lids on her cases, she thought how a tiger beetle would have been just the thing to round out her general display case. However, many more aquatic insects were needed for the second case. She had especially hoped to snag several species of dragonflies. But now...

If only the Vandynes were moving in without a tall, handsome football player in tow, the situation wouldn't be so complicated. She'd simply walk up to the elegant double doors, give a bold knock, and request permission to continue using the grounds as before.

But Spence. Spence messed up everything. From what Cissy and Winnie said—and if their opinion was true—there wouldn't be a chance in a million she could spend time at Kendallwood on an insect hunt without being hounded by every girl at Andonburg High. It was time to face facts. Her days of building displays from the garden and pond at Kendallwood were over, and she despised the letdown she was feeling. She leaned back in her chair and gave a deep sigh.

Would Spence think her odd if he knew about her? Would he call her Bug Brain like all the other guys? She thought again of his easy laugh and his sense of humor. She smiled as she remembered his remark about not letting his coach get word of that *tackle*. A witty remark.

And when he called her *pint-sized* he'd made it sound as if being short wasn't so bad, even though at times her small size left her feeling insignificant.

He'd helped her up too. None of the guys in Andonburg were that polite. She wondered if Spence could possibly be as big-headed about his football status as Dub Weston.

Dub held the status of the star of the Andonburg Antelopes, and his brash attitude disgusted Marcy. He was a regular at the drug store since he came in to check on *his* girl—as he referred to Cissy.

Marcy turned off the light and closed the workroom door behind her. One thing she was sure of, Dub Weston would never reach down and help a girl to her feet. Dub would have laughed his head off.

Maybe she was a Bug Brain like everyone said, but she wasn't blind. She could see there was something decidedly different about Spence Caldwell.

5

Chapter Five

The sun was spreading flecks of gold through the lemon-yellow Pricilla curtains of the twins' bedroom when Marcy awoke the next morning. Thoughts of losing access to Kendallwood were set aside as she remembered today marked the arrival of the shipment of school supplies at the store. When the initial school supplies came in, every member of the family pitched in to help unload, sort, mark merchandise, and stock the shelves.

Aromas of coffee drifting into her room announced that her parents were up and about. Across the room Cissy snuggled down deeper into her covers until only a wisp or two of her sandy hair peeked out.

With no wasted motions, Marcy slipped from her bed, grabbed her pink slacks and matching blouse from the closet and headed to the bathroom to dress. As she plugged in the curling iron to touch up her short hair, she remembered the thrill she'd always felt as a child when the school supplies arrived. As they unpacked the crayons, erasers, bottles of glue, colorful pencil boxes, and notebooks, she felt she had an edge over every other kid in town. Years passed before she discovered most of the kids didn't care one whit if the stuff never came in!

She was smoothing out the quilt on her bed and fluffing pillows when Cissy sat up with a low moan. "If you wouldn't get in such an all-fired hurry, you wouldn't make me look so bad." Cissy punctuated the words with a wide yawn. "How can you be so anxious to go down there and attack those brontosaurus-sized boxes?"

Marcy smiled at her twin. "It has to be done." She fluffed the last pillow and turned to go.

"Delightful philosophy." Cissy stretched with another groan. "Simply delightful."

Marcy had no words to describe her feelings to her sister, who always accused Marcy of being too serious-minded. While wrestling big boxes wasn't that enjoyable, it was the sensation of the finished results that she loved. In her opinion, their store was the most attractive one on Main Street, and the neatly stocked shelves added the special touch.

"There comes our eager beaver," her father said looking up from the morning newspaper. His wide smile made crinkle lines appear above his high cheekbones. Alan Hankins' tall frame gave him an Abe Lincoln look with dark hair and his loose-jointed walk.

From across the kitchen her mother pointed to a platter stacked with steaming pancakes. "Butter those, would you please, Marcy?" The box of pancake mix on the cabinet near the stove let Marcy know her mother was in a hurry, as though hurried preparations would give a kick-start to those around her. Marcy smiled. It'd take more than a quick breakfast to light a fire under Cissy.

Her mother's short, slim figure decked out in Levis and cotton shirt gave her the look of a teenager. For better or for worse, Marcy had inherited her mother's petite size while Cissy was lanky like their father.

Not turning from the griddle, her mother said, "Alan, should we take Marcy to the store with us and let Cissy finish up here? Or the other way around?"

The newspaper lowered as Alan started to answer, but Reta didn't notice. "Or should we wait a few minutes and herd the whole bunch with us. That way, it'll guarantee no dawdling on the part of those left behind. Sometimes..." She paused as she surveyed a rumple-haired Bernie who had just wandered into the kitchen. "Sometimes, some people can't be trusted to do their chores and come on down to the store quickly when he's left behind."

Bernie rubbed his eyes and yawned. Marcy knew that even more than Cissy, Bernie dreaded the unloading.

"Aw Mom, I'm the only guy in town who has to slave away working instead of playing all summer."

"You have your days off," their mother reminded him.

Alan's response wasn't quite as gentle. "Bernard Alan Hankins, you have exactly ten minutes to get your hair combed, your teeth brushed, your clothes on and your breakfast eaten! Now get a move on."

Bernie was out the door and down the hall before the command was finished. And after Reta's third call, Cissy was also up.

"Now to answer your question, Mrs. Hankins," Alan said as he folded his newspaper and turned his attention to the pancakes in front of him, "the truck is due in early. I'll take Marcy with me and you ride herd on the other two and join us as quickly as you can."

Reta laughed as she sat down beside him. "Good thinking, Boss. It's a deal." They slapped a high five making Marcy laugh.

Later, as Marcy left the house with her father, she felt a twinge of embarrassment that she was always the available one. Cissy often accused Marcy of doing it on purpose to make her twin look bad, but that wasn't true. Perhaps deep down, Cissy really knew it wasn't true. Marcy could only hope so.

By late morning, the work flowed smoothly with a minimum of interruptions from customers. Bernie was, by then, out making a few pharmacy deliveries and their parents were in the back room discussing ideas for special displays and sales features when Winnie Denton came in. Cissy immediately dropped her work to wait on her friend.

Winnie ordered a Coke, and over the yellow counter the two began talking about the hottest news—Spence Caldwell. Excitedly, they inquired if the other had seen him yet, or talked to anyone who had. When that fact was established in the negative, talk turned to the newcomer's football aspirations.

"Seems impossible he'd go out for football with a puny little team like ours, doesn't it?" Winnie chewed on her straw and she pondered the thought. "I mean, after having played with such a big high school team? Maybe he won't go out for football at all."

"Nonsense," Cissy retorted, "you've read all the news articles. Why the guy lives and breathes footfall. He'll be our star player for sure. We'll be the envy of every other town in the county." Cissy wiped off the counter in the same place with a wet cloth, leaning close to Winnie so they could talk softly. It was against their parents' rules for the girls to visit with friends during work hours.

Cissy went on. "This is going to be the most exciting year ever for Andonburg High. And if we work it right, Winnie, we'll be right in the middle of all the excitement."

Marcy stacked spiral notebooks according to sizes and wondered what Cissy mean by that comment. She knew from experience there was no telling which direction her twin's mind might go next.

"Marcy and I will be able to *twin up* with our hair before long. Hers is nearly grown out so we'll be able to French braid it by the time school begins."

Marcy stood up and looked over the gondola at her sister. With both hands she ruffled up her short hair and made a silly face. "It's *my* hair, don't forget," she declared. It wasn't fair for Cissy to talk about her hair as if it didn't even belong to her.

"You didn't have to cut it *so* short." Cissy raised her hand as if to throw the wet cloth across the room at Marcy. She held the pose and gave her sister a scowl before returning to the gossip session.

Cissy enjoyed playing up the twin bit to the hilt; Marcy wanted to be her own person. She figured the only reason Cissy did it was to get attention. At the close of the school year last spring Marcy set up a secret appointment at Betty's Beauty Box to get her hair cut short. Her mother was shocked, Cissy was furious, Bernie could have cared less. It was her father who stated that she had the right to wear her hair in any style she wished. It was amazing to her now that Cissy would be planning hair styles and school was still weeks away.

The marking gun Marcy was using on the notebooks was giving her fits, and she stopped work to adjust it. As she fiddled with it, she was thinking of some way to get Cissy back to work before her parents caught her and the whole place would be in an uproar. In a few minutes the sticky little price labels were coming forth in proper order, and she slapped prices of the last of the stack of notebooks.

"Cissy," she said picking up the empty box in which the notebooks had been shipped, "I have a great idea for dressing the front window. What to hear?" Her twin didn't look too receptive, but the comment seemed to break up the jam session.

Winnie hopped down from the counter stool. "I know you girls have work to do. Truth is, I do too. Mother's waiting for me to help her cut out skirt patterns for the little ones. Actually, I came in for a spool of thread."

The *little ones* to whom Winnie referred were her three younger, red-headed sisters who kept her nearly as busy as the drug store did the twins. After she made her purchase and left, Cissy came over to where Marcy was breaking down boxes. "So, what's the great idea?"

"Remember the muslin-covered frames stored in the back room?"

"The ones Dad used Christmas-before-last as a backdrop for the nativity scene?"

"Yeah. Those. Let's use them for a backdrop again – putting them up in the far window. We could get one of the old wooden side-arm school desks that Mr. Walsh keeps stored in the building behind the high school. We'll paint it fire-engine red, then make the window look like an old-fashioned school room. "

She waited a minute, weighing out here twin's reception. It was the moment of suspense, not knowing what Cissy might categorize as work and flatly refuse. Cissy silently lifted her long hair up off her neck, thinking.

Marcy went on before a *no* could be spoken. "We could mount a black poster board on the frame to look like a blackboard. On it we'll write what specials Mom and Dad are running that week."

Now Cissy's eyes brightened. "And then, how about setting one of the bar stools from home over in the corner with a dunce hat perched on it?"

Bingo. Marcy scored again.

"Plus," Cissy added, "fetching the desk and painting it would get us out of this place for a while."

Together they formulated several more ideas, then presented them to their father. For the most part, Alan encouraged the girls' creativity in the store, anxious for them to take an interest in all facets of the business. This was no exception. The idea of a schoolroom display in the front window, he said, was a super-great idea.

6

Chapter Six

After lunch, the girls trekked up to the high school. Everything in the town of Andonburg—being so close to the Arkansas border—was in one of two directions. Up or down. The high school building was situated on a hill to the east of town, just a few blocks south of the road that led out of town toward the Kendallwood estate.

The three-story stone edifice had changed little since their mother attended years ago. The recent addition of the sprawling one-story structure in the back provided added classroom space and a bit of a modern touch; but the original building stood proud and undaunted on the brow in the hill like an ancient fortress.

Their father called ahead to talk to the snowy-haired Mr. Walsh, whose gruff exterior belied a heart of gold. Marcy had heard her father speaking forcefully on the phone since Mr. Walsh was a trifle hard of hearing. "Say, Mr. Walsh. I'm looking to buy one of those old side-arm desks. You got one for sale?"

Equally loud, the girls could hear the reply coming from the other end. "Land sakes, Hankins, if you want to come and take some of them off my hands, I'd be eternally grateful. They're taking up so consarned much room now, I ain't got no room for nothing else. And them school board members won't let me get rid of 'em."

And so, the spritely Mr. Walsh met the girls at the school, making a fuss because they were out walking in the mid-day heat bare-headed. With strong steps led them out to the large metal storage shed. "No sense you girls coming in here. It's hotter than the hubs of Hades in that thing."

They heard a lot of clattering and banging, after which he came out carrying one of the antique desks. Cissy promptly sat down in it. "Yuck. This thing is like sitting on a board. It'd be pure torture to sit in this all day."

"Let me try."

Cissy moved out of the way and with a sweep of the hand motioned for Marcy to have a seat.

"You're right. It's awful. Obviously designed as a torture machine from a medieval torture dungeon," she commented, bringing giggles from Cissy.

"Hey," Mr. Walsh said. "How'd you like to have had to sit on a split log bench with no back like my grandpappy did?" Waving toward the chair, he added, "Old grandpappy woulda thought this here desk was mighty comfy."

Thoughtfully, Marcy traced her fingers over the tiny valleys of carved initials in the worn desk top and reflected on the students from bygone years who carved them there. Perhaps her mother's initials were etched somewhere among the stacks of old dusty relics. It would have undoubtedly read: "WWW loves RJL."

She and Cissy knew well the story of how young W. W. Weston (Dub's father) had dated Reta all through high school. But as chance would have it, on a visit to her aunt's in Chicago the summer after graduation, Reta met the young pharmaceutical college student, Alan Hankins. The two were married before the year was out, much to the chagrin of young Weston who had believed Reta Lamont was all his.

Now, ironically, Dub, Jr. evoked the same smug sureness about his relationship with Cissy. Like father, like son, Marcy mused to herself.

Just then, Cissy ran off into the main building to get a drink which gave Marcy the moment she needed to ask Mr. Walsh about the surprise arrival of the Vandyne family.

His answer, however, was no help at all. "I was just as surprised as the next fella. I never got no word they was a-coming. A hasty decision they made, I'd say." He closed the door to the storage building and clicked the padlock into place. "The missus there give me leave of my work for now. For which I'm purely grateful. Too much for an old fella like me to keep up."

Seeing Cissy coming out the door of the school, she cut off the conversation. She sure didn't want her sister asking prying questions about the Vandynes. "Well, Mr. Walsh," she said raising her voice some, "thanks so much for getting us the desk. We've got to get back now. Come on Cissy. Help me with this thing."

The August air hung in a thick, humid curtain as they carried the desk between them back down the hill to Main Street. Their hair clung to their faces and necks in patchy curls. The buzzing of insects indicated that the bugs, at least, had retained a measure of energy.

"The people in this block will think we're nuts," Marcy said, struggling with her end of the bulky desk.

"I'm tired already. Let's set it down a minute and rest." Cissy weakly placed herself in the desk seat the moment it touched the ground.

Laughing, Marcy plopped down in the grass under a shade tree. "You look crazy. Wish I had my camera."

They both giggled until Cissy suddenly sobered. "Oh no! Here comes Maureen Ratherfield, of all people. And driving her daddy's big car too."

The long Cadillac, prize possession of Andonburg's one and only attorney, pulled smoothly to a stop by the curb. The automatic car window slid down smoothly and the girls could feel the rush of cool air blowing from the car's interior. They knew of few people in town whose car came equipped with air conditioning. Or automatic windows.

"Hi y'all," she called to them. Maureen's shiny black hair was pulled back from her face held with a gauzy flowered scarf, giving her a fresh, cool appearance. "Do y'all always carry your own chair when you go for a walk?" She chuckled at her own lame joke.

Not getting up, Cissy said, "Only when it's hot, Maureen."

Ignoring the clipped answer, Maureen went on to more important matters. "Did y'all hear about Spence coming to town?"

Marcy could feel her twin tensing up at the mention of her new heartthrob. The heartthrob she'd yet to meet. The first-name basis with which Maureen referred to him made it sound as though the two were already friends, but Marcy was reasonably sure that was impossible. There simply hadn't been time. She got up and stepped closer to the car.

"Yes, we've heard the news. He's living at Kendallwood, right?"

"Uh huh. At the estate." Maureen's words flowed smooth as honey, or so Cissy often accused. Her family had hailed from Georgia several years earlier, and the girl just never seemed to lose her strong southern accent. "You know, Daddy's been handling their estate for several years now and we're just so excited that Spence's aunt and uncle are coming to restore the old place. It'll be such a lovely asset to Andonburg's quaintness. Don't you agree?"

Since her question didn't require an answer, she continued. "Mama and Daddy have decided to throw a big old party at our house to welcome them to our fair little city. Won't that just be the sweetest thing to do?" She waved her crimson-tipped nails through the air as she spoke.

Cissy sat stone-faced and said nothing. Marcy felt the discomfort of the silence. "Why has Spence Caldwell come to Andonburg anyway?" she asked. "Weren't college football scouts keeping an eye on him?" Of course, Marcy didn't know any of this; she'd just heard Winnie talking about it.

"We don't really know," Maureen admitted. "Daddy never knew Fred and Daisy even had a nephew, let alone his being a famous high school football star, until just a few weeks ago. That was the day they phoned Daddy to say they were moving here. Isn't it all just *so* interesting?"

Maureen's voice was as fluttery as her hand gestures.

"If I learn any juicy little tidbits, you two girls will be the first ones to know. I promise." Her green eyes grew wide. "Maybe he's an heir to all the Kendallwood millions, but only if he agrees to live on bread and water in the turret of the old house during football season in Andonburg, Oklahoma."

Her lilting laughter floated on the steamy August air—steaming Cissy more with each passing moment.

"But just you never mind. I'll find out all about it next Saturday night at our party. Well, I really must be getting along now. Catch you girls later." She gave a baby wave and whirred up the window as the car pulled away.

"It'll be such a luv-lay asset to Andonburg's quaintness," Cissy mocked in exaggerated slurs, sweeping her hand grandly in front of her face. "You two guhrls will be the fuhst ones to heah." Cissy slapped at the desk top. "I'll just bet. Any information she learns about Spence she'll share only with the teddy bear she sleeps with."

"Come on now, Cissy. Maureen's not that bad."

"No? Then tell me why that girl gets everything? And I mean *everything*!" Cissy stood and picked up her end of the desk. "Remember when we were in junior high and her mother drove her to Tulsa every week for dance lessons?"

As Marcy took the other end of the desk, and as they started back down the sidewalk, Cissy kept up her rant. "That girl always has the best clothes, the best looks, and the most money. And now she gets to meet Spence Caldwell first at a party at her very own house. It just isn't fair."

Marcy swiped damp hair from her cheek and wondered what Cissy would say if she knew her very own twin had actually met Spence first?

Truthfully, she didn't even want to know.

Chapter Seven

Marcy came out the back door of the store into the alleyway with an armful of old newspapers. Dropping the stack onto the ground she unfolded each one and spread them out as a shield against the red paint. Meanwhile, Cissy was inside gathering paint and brushes.

As she worked, Marcy thought over what Cissy had said about Maureen. She had to admit that Maureen was loaded with more of life's blessings than most of their friends. Add to that the fact that most of the guys in school were nuts about her, which also frustrated Cissy. In spite of it all, Marcy didn't want to see her sister get bogged down in petty jealousy. But then, who was she to point fingers? After all, didn't she envy Cissy's ability to carry on a conversation and be the life of the party in every situation?

The slamming of the door broke into her thoughts. "Here we are," Cissy called out, holding up the paint can. "Red as red can be. Just what you ordered."

The two had changed into old clothes kept in the backroom for cleaning days, and both donned red bandanas to keep paint from getting in their hair. As they set to work, the soggy heat gave Marcy second thoughts about her idea which had sounded so great inside the air-conditioned store. The only solution was to work quickly and get back in out of the heat as soon as possible.

"Look out," she spouted at Cissy, wiping paint from her arm. "You splattered me."

"Well la te da, Marcy Hankins. You won't die from a drip of paint, you know." With that Cissy gave her brush a flick, spraying drips down the leg of Marcy's faded Levi's—on purpose this time.

"Oh, so that's how it is. This means war, you foul, evil cad." Marcy jumped back away from the desk and held up her paint brush like a sword.

Cissy picked up the refrain. "No, no. Pray thee, give me a bit of mercy, you heartless tyrant. I shall avenge my honor to the end." She hopped to her feet, placed one arm behind her back, and thrust out the brush as though it were a sword.

Marcy squared off. "Dost thou fair prince dare to think he can avenge himself of this unthinkable offence? I dare say thou shalt lose thy kingdom, thy honor, and thy life!"

"Verily, me thinks thou are quite yellow down thy not-so-fair back. Dare thee insult the prince of the entire kingdom?" Cissy moved in to make a sharp thrust. Letting out a squeal, Marcy jumped aside just in time.

"Thou didst miss, thou clumsy fool." As Marcy side-stepped, she whirled around and deftly jabbed her sister in the side with her brush. "Touché," she yelled, laughing. "Behold how the yellow prince doth bleed red."

Suddenly a voice behind them caused them both to freeze.

"Wonderful fencing. The dastardly prince didn't deserve a bit of mercy."

Marcy whirled about and was shocked to see Spence standing there big as life, his dimples creased in a huge grin. He was clapping at their alleyway performance. She felt almost as ridiculous as then they took their tumble together in the driveway at Kendallwood. Holding her breath, she hoped he wouldn't even recognize her in this getup.

Now he was looking around as if he'd lost something. "So, where's the guard dog that attacks?" He shot a glance at Marcy. She looked away so as not to meet his gaze.

"You're Spence Caldwell, aren't you." This firm statement from Cissy who had recovered her dignity in a split second. "I recognize you from your pictures in the paper." She reached up to straighten her bandana and, in the process, managed to add another streak of red to her cheek.

"I'm honored to be recognized." He gave a silly little bow.

"I'm Cissy Hankins, Spence." She transferred the brush to her left hand and extended her paint-splattered right one for a hand shake. "This is my twin, Marcy," she added, nodding toward Marcy. "And we don't own a guard dog."

"Your twin there had a ferocious guard dog up at Kendallwood yesterday that nearly took my left off." He rubbed his chin as though searching his memory. "Let's see now... It was some kind of terrifying name. Bitsy? Wasn't that it? Bitsy?"

Cissy gave her sister a cold stare.

"Yes. Bitsy." Marcy's voice was small.

"You two have met?" Cissy glanced from one to the other.

"Only momentarily. You could say we just sort of ran into each other." With that, he gave a soft chuckle.

The buildings along the alley stood as barriers against any breeze that chanced to be moving. To Marcy, the August heat had intensified to that of a furnace. She stepped closer to the desk, placing her hand on an unpainted portion to steady herself. Fainting dead away wouldn't be too impressive either.

8

Chapter Eight

"Sorry to barge in like this," Spence was saying, "but my Aunt Daisy sent me to pick up some empty boxes. Someone told me to check out the drug store. So, I came around to the back looking for boxes. But which one's the drug store? All these doors look alike to me."

Cissy rallied in a heartbeat, evidently determined not to let this golden opportunity slip through her fingers. "This is the right place, and it's the right time to get boxes." Her voice grew more animated as she lay her brush down across the top of the open paint can. "Our family just finished the gruesome task of unloading a shipment of merchandise this morning and we are blessed with an ample supply. How many do you need?"

Marcy stood there amazed that Cissy could be so at ease when she looked a fright. As Cissy busied herself gaining the upper hand in the conversation, Marcy dipped her brush and returned to the work at hand.

"Just need a few," Spence answered. "Aunt Daisy's in a tizzy trying to decide what to keep out and what to store until the remodeling is finished."

The word *remodeling* snapped into Marcy's subconscious. It hadn't occurred to her that the Vandynes might possibly change the Kendallwood house. Perhaps Daisy Vandyne was the type who would paint over the old stained woodwork in bright colors, and redo the house using modern designs. She stared at her dripping brush. Restoration, yes. But remodeling? She hoped not.

But what business was it of hers what the Vandynes did with their inheritance? Nothing she could do about it.

She glanced up just as Cissy led the way into the back door to direct Spence to the boxes which they had broken down and stacked in a back room. Breathlessly, she tried to remember if the door was closed to her entomology workroom. At the same moment she scolded herself for such a panicked reaction. Perhaps she was more weary than she had realized at all the off-handed comments about her work.

When the two emerged from the store, Cissy was still gaily chattering, asking all sorts of mundane questions to keep the conversation going.

"Come help us," Cissy called from behind an armload of boxes that were about to slip out of her arms.

Spence shook his head, dropping his armload. "No, that's all right. I'll just drive my car down the alley and then pick them up." Cissy smiled up at him as he took the stack from her. "That is, if it's not illegal to drive and park in the alley."

Now Cissy gave a light twittery laugh, which sounded similar to Maureen's. "Remember, Mr. Caldwell," she said, "this isn't Oklahoma City. It's perfectly legal to drive up and down the alleys of Andonburg to your heart's desire."

In a moment, Spence returned in the gorgeous Corvette that left Cissy practically in shock. She stepped up quickly to hand him boxes and assist in cramming them into the small car.

"I guess you're anxious to start football practice with our guys." She let the open-ended question sort of float out on the air.

Marcy found herself straining to hear his reply. Marcy Hankins, probably the only non-sports-minded individual in the whole town. Even she had been stirred by thoughts of having a winning team for a change. There was, however, a moment of silence while Spence chose to adjust boxes to fit in the car rather than comment.

Cissy tried again, this time more discreet. "Well, I could understand if you didn't want to play alongside the Andonburg Antelopes. After all, we're a far cry from the team you're used to. I guess everyone would understand."

"Sorry." Spence turned to face Cissy. Marcy could see his smile. "I didn't mean to be secretive. Yes, I am ready to get back into practice. And it'll be a pleasure to support the guys from your school. It won't be that much different from the school I came from. After all, football is football."

His last words were stilted and unconvincing, but Marcy could tell Cissy hadn't caught it. Her sister was so excited she could have leaped over the Corvette in a single bound.

"That's such a great attitude, Spence," Cissy managed to say. "I know all the guys are more than ready to have you out there on the field with them." Then, in her cute way, Cissy thrust out her paint-stained hand and said, "We just want to extend to you a formal welcome to our fair little city of Andonburg, Spence."

Spence took her hand, thanked her, then piled his large frame into the small car. After taking a moment to include a wave and smile toward Marcy, he drove away.

Marcy braced herself as Cissy turned on her with a vengeance. "You traitor! How could you? I cannot believe you did that to me. You actually met him and never even told me. When I asked you, you refused to tell me. It's so unfair. You knew how important it was for me to know everything about him."

Taking a deep breath, Marcy tried to think quick. "I'm sorry, Cissy. Really, I am. It was an embarrassing incident. Bitsy got loose from me and I made a fool of myself. I didn't think you would want to hear that your twin made an unfavorable first impression. And besides all that, I just grabbed Bitsy and left in a hurry. I sure didn't do it to hurt you."

"Well, what's done is done, I suppose. After all, I know you don't think about boys like I do. It was nothing to you to meet him. It's just that I wanted to know what he looked like up close. But *now* I know!" Cissy's eyes gazed off dreamily. "Oh Marcy, he's more, more, and a thousand times more than I had ever hoped he would be. That build; those enchanting dimples. And so thoughtful." She turned back to Marcy now. "Did you see how he helped me with the boxes?"

As if running out of steam, Cissy sat down near the nearly-finished desk. "But you could have at least told me how big and handsome he was." Then after a moment, she added. "Oh, Marcy, isn't it so exciting that I got to meet him first after all. Maureen will be furious!"

Suddenly she leaped to her feet. "You can finish up here, can't you? It's almost done anyway."

"Why? Where're you going?"

At the back door now, she called over her shoulder, "To see if I can sneak a quick phone call to Winnie without getting caught."

Later as Marcy washed the brushes at the outside faucet, her sister reappeared. She'd made the transfer from totally giddy to quiet and thoughtful. Marcy wasn't sure which was more dangerous.

"Somehow we've got to keep Maureen from getting cheerleader this year," was all she said.

"What? Where did that come from?"

"Winnie and I have talked it over..."

Marcy took that to mean the secret phone call had been a success.

"...and we have it all figured out."

"That's nice." Marcy flicked water from the brushes and laid them out to dry on the newspapers.

"No, listen. This is important. This includes you. I'm going to need your help."

"My help? Why my help?"

"Remember last year in the tryouts, Maureen and I ran neck-and-neck in the competition."

"I remember."

"Now Selena Thomas is in the picture."

"So?" Selena was a senior who had moved to Andonburg last spring.

"I happen to know that Selena was head cheerleader in the school she moved from. I've seen her and she's terrific. She knows all kinds of neat routines."

Marcy hated riddles and wished her sister would get to the point. She started picking up the newspapers, wadded them in a big ball and put them in the nearby dumpster. "That has nothing to do with me."

"Just listen and you'll understand. The way Winnie and I see it, Selena, Winnie and I will win for varsity cheerleaders. Now if you *twin up* with me and tryout as well, Maureen will be squeezed out completely."

Marcy was already shaking her head as she dragged the desk over closer to the back door. But Cissy wasn't deterred.

"Maureen will be up in the stands during football season and I'll be down on the field where the action is. How does that sound?"

"Awful. Now help me get this inside. We've got to change and get that window finished. I don't even want to talk about anything even remotely related to cheerleading or football."

Suddenly Cissy was by her side opening the door. "Here let me help you with that. I love your idea about the window. We'll get it fixed up in no time at all."

As usual, Cissy had no thought of letting the matter drop. As they worked in the front window, she said, "I think a change of pace is just was the doctor ordered in the life of a serious-minded person like you." Cissy drew spelling words on one of the black poster boards in a childish scrawl. "It's downright dangerous for you to spend so much time in that stuffy old room back there. You're liable to mummify. You could spring a leak in a kill jar and be asphyxiated." She shook her head and made a mournful expression. "Bad news. Bad, bad news."

Keeping a straight face around Cissy was impossible. It certainly wouldn't be the first time she'd been conned into doing something entirely for Cissy' benefit. Rather than resenting it, Marcy simply accepted it as part of her sister's personality.

But now that the idea had been introduced, she couldn't help but think about it. In junior high, she and Cissy had been cheerleaders together. But that was before she "went off the deep end," as Cissy described her entomology work.

Getting back into the swing of being a cheerleader might be fun. But she had to be honest with herself. It would drastically cut into her research time. Practice would be demanding, since it had been a while since her short legs had done the splits, high kicks, and cartwheels. She was rusty and she knew it.

Maybe she did need a change of pace. After all, she mused as she arranged a pencil box on the red desk, it really wouldn't hurt anything to let up a little on the entomology. It wasn't really that pressing. She had wanted so much to win Grand Champion at the county fair, but losing access to Kendallwood put a damper on that dream.

"And you need the exercise too." Cissy's stream of ceaseless chatter continued. "You need exercise *and* excitement. The time to live is when you're young. How will you feel if you look back years from now and all you remember about your high school years is that you played with *bugs?*"

Marcy only half-listened as she imagined what would have happened if the door to her workroom was open when Cissy and Spence went after the boxes. She could just hear Cissy saying something like, "Oh ignore that room. That's where Marcy goes to shut herself up with creepy crawly things. Ugh! It stinks in there. We try to keep the door shut at all times!"

She put her fingers to her temples and pressed hard. *If I truly believe in my research with the insects, and if I'm going to make it my life's work, why does it matter what Cissy, or Spence, or anyone else thinks about it?*

She stared out at the street of her hometown. Few people were moving about in the oppressive heat.

It did make a difference though. No matter how much she wished it didn't, it *did* make a difference what people thought.

9

Chapter Nine

Tryouts loomed only a few days away. Agonizing aching in Marcy's legs and back gave her strong doubts that she would ever be ready.

"Please, let's rest just a minute," she begged, stretching out on the cool grass under the maple tree in the vacant lot down the street from their house.

Winnie walked over and looked down, gazing directly at Marcy. "Don't stop now," she pleaded. "You almost had it that last time. It's just that you keep missing the hop-clap on the offbeat. You can get it if you keep trying. I know you can."

"I hurt too much," Marcy said with a groan, then closed her eyes against Winnie's encouraging smile above her.

"Aw, let her rest," Cissy broke in. "It's been years since she's had to be nimble-footed." She flopped down beside her twin. "Guess the rheumatiz' has set in, eh, Granny?"

Marcy felt a playful jab in her side, but she didn't open her eyes. "Call it what you like. All I know is that I hurt. All over."

Reluctantly, Winnie joined them on the grass, but continued in her chosen role as their coach. "You'll get the kinks out if you don't give up," she said, sounding more like a mother than a friend. She picked up the paper with the cheers listed on it and reviewed the ones they had yet to practice that evening, as though it were impermissible to let up even for a few minutes.

The three of them had been practicing in the vacant lot nearly every evening since Marcy had said *yes* to Cissy and Winnie's plan. It was what they'd been begging to hear, and Cissy said over and over again that this was going to be the most exciting year ever for Andonburg High School.

"Rest time's over." Winnie jumped to her feet and moved into formation for another cheer. Cissy fell in beside her and Marcy painfully managed to hoist herself up off the ground and force her body to take yet another step.

⁺·⁺ ° ♡ ° ⁺·⁺

Marcy arrived at the house just as the lavender streaks were fading from the sky and the mosquitoes had appeared. While Winnie and Cissy stayed out on the porch to talk about their cheerleader uniforms, Marcy went in looking forward to a soaking bath to ease her aches and pains. She found her mother in the kitchen.

"Marcy, you look terrible. Your face is flushed and you're sweating like a race horse." Her mother scooted out a chair, into which Marcy collapsed. "Don't you think you're overdoing this cheerleading thing a bit?" She stepped to the refrigerator and fixed a glass of ice water for her daughter.

Marcy took a long drink. "Thanks, Mom. I guess I'm more out of shape than I thought. Those two don't know the meaning of the word *quit.* Or *rest* either for that matter." She managed a weak smile as her mother sat down in the chair opposite her.

"Forgive me, but I don't understand all of this." Her mother looked directly into her eyes. "How are you going to have time for this cheerleading business, plus your homework once school starts, plus helping out in the store, plus your entomology projects?"

Each *plus* gained not so much in volume as it did in strong emphasis. Although Reta Hankins seldom raised her voice, she had a manner which was quite direct.

Marcy tried not to squirm under the close scrutiny, because she'd been asking herself the same questions repeatedly. With no real answers.

"For one thing," she said slowly, "once we're into school and into the season, we won't be practicing every night. This is just for tryouts. And I might not even make it. Who knows?" She drank the last of the ice water, stalling while she collected her thoughts. "As for my entomology, the cases are nearly ready for the fair. As ready as they'll ever be now that I've lost access to Kendallwood."

The reality of her loss was growing on Marcy with each passing day. She felt herself sink a little as she verbalized it.

"Why, Marcy, I'd be willing to bet that Mr. and Mrs. Vandyne wouldn't mind if you continued to use the grounds like before. You've certainly not bothering anyone. How about if I call and ask them?"

"I'm afraid it's not that simple."

"What do you mean?"

"Spence," she said as if that told it all.

"The nephew? The football player? What's he got to do with it?"

Marcy heaved a sigh. "It's just that every girl in Andonburg is in a dither over him. If I were to spend time there now, every female in the whole school would hound me relentlessly. My sister being one of them. And no one, I repeat *no one* would believe I was there looking for insects."

"I see." Her mother seemed to be processing this new information. "How would it be if your father and I called around to see if we can locate another place for your work? Surely Kendallwood is not the only spot around with a pond and underbrush."

"It's no use, Mom." She hated the sound of despair in her voice. It seemed so melodramatic. "Kendallwood was so close and so. So..." Right words failed her. *Deserted* came to mind. But it sounded so redundant she left the sentence dangling.

"But I've been thinking," she went on using a different tack, "that maybe I've been working too hard anyway. Perhaps my life has been off balance. Everyone seems to think that I never have any fun." She tossed the thoughts out that she'd been loath to express before. With the possibility of become a cheerleader looming in front of her, it seemed almost safe to say them.

Her mother was quiet again. Then, "The cheerleading is fine, Marcy. Nothing wrong with it, if that's what your heart is set on doing. Just be careful that you're not doing it simply because you were talked into it. Because if you are, you'll be miserable."

Resentment flared suddenly at the insinuation that she was so susceptible to Cissy's influence. "I *wasn't* talked into it," she said. "It's just that I've made up my mind to have some fun for a change. Is that a crime?"

She moved quickly to get up from the table, forgetting for a moment that her legs now had a mind of their own, and she nearly fell back down into the chair.

"Fun?" her mother asked giving her a gentle pat.

Marcy jerked away and headed down the hall to the bathroom for a long soaking bath.

Chapter Ten

The twins received many compliments on their original window display. As the beginning of school grew ever nearer, mothers descended on the store waving pink slips issued by the school listing supplies needed for each grade level. Marcy was filling just such an order for a harried mother surrounded by several barefoot youngsters when Cissy sidled up to her.

"Let me take over for you," she said softly. "I just saw Dub drive up. I need you to go wait on him."

Marcy hesitated. She couldn't walk off and turn over a customer to Cissy. That was not how their parents had taught them to conduct business.

"Please?" Cissy mouthed in mock panic as the customer's back was turned.

Marcy was about to give in when their father called from back in the pharmacy. "Cissy, you're needed at the fountain."

Cissy rolled her eyes and clenched her fists. "No mercy," she whispered. "No mercy at all."

Cissy was scooping ice cream into a cone for a little boy when Dub burst through the front door. Marcy rang up the school order at the checkout counter, watching as the drama unfolded. Dub, dressed in his usual Levis and western shirt, scanned the store till he saw Cissy at the fountain and his eyes lit up.

He reminded Marcy of the hero of a Western movie standing at the swinging doors of the saloon, surveying the place before swaggering in the door. Dub was nearly the size of Spence and was the spitting image of his rancher-father, W. W. Weston, famous for miles around for his prize Charolais cattle.

"Howdy, there, Cissy." Dub gave an exaggerated wave with an oversized hand as though Cissy had failed to see him.

Their mother often said she held her breath when Dub came into the store. "He moves like a young bull calf," she'd say, "with uncontrolled energy shooting out in uneven spurts."

"When you're done with that little guy there," he said in his equally over-sized voice, "fix me an orange soda with lots of ice. It's plumb hot out there."

"Sure, Dub," Cissy said in her friendliest tone. Probably so that their father would hear and take note.

Dub's boots made a scuffing noise as he seated himself at the counter. "I hear tell you're going all out on your cheerleading practice, Cissy. You must be counting on the team doing great this season if you're working that hard at it."

Marcy finished with her customer and joined Cissy at the fountain cleaning around the ice cream wells, mildly aware of the peculiar twinge of curiosity of what he had to say about the team. "You're out there practicing in the hot sun, Dub," she cut into the conversation. "Tell us how it looks for the year."

Dub turned his tanned face toward her as though seeing her for the first time. His mischievous eyes were alive with amusement. "What's this? Did Professor Hankins come out of her bug laboratory and ask a question about the football team? He slapped his knee and gave a phony laugh. "What's this world coming to?"

Marcy scrubbed harder at the spilled spots of ice cream, bracing herself to allow the sting of his remark to subside. Would she never get used to this type of teasing even after hearing it for so long?

This time, Cissy rose stiffly to her sister's defense. "For your information Dub Weston, Marcy and I are *both* trying out for cheerleader this year. So, watch your remarks." She set his soda in front of him with a little bang which sent a spray of the bright orange drink out onto the counter.

"Well now," he continued, "won't that be a real treat to have both the Hankins out there cheering me on to victory. I'm honored for sure."

"How *is* the team shaping up," Cissy asked more intently. "You never answered Marcy's question.

"Super," was all he said, then took a long drink from the soda. Marcy kept washing down the ice cream wells, and Cissy wiped orange spots off the counter. He seemed he was going to say more. They waited.

Finally, he added, "If only that Caldwell guy hadn't come hogging his way in. Thinks he's so hot just 'cause he's played on a big Oklahoma City team, and 'cause all those college scouts are after him." His expression turned into a sneer. "The guy gives me a real pain."

"A pain?" Cissy's voice rose to a near squeak. "You should be thankful for the know-how he'll be adding to our team, Dub Weston. Shame on you! We're lucky to be getting him. We'll be the envy of the entire county."

"Aw, who needs him? We were doing okay without him." Dub drained the last of his soda making loud slurping noises.

The twinkle was gone from his eyes which caused a tiny shiver to run up Marcy's back.

"Tell you something else," Dub went on. "If that big shot keeps throwing his weight around, I'll just have to whip him right along with the opposing team. And I'm just the one who can do it." Pushing his glass away from him, he added, "A city slicker's all he is."

By this time, Cissy looked angry enough to throw something. Marcy stepped over and put her hand on her sister's arm. At that moment their mother emerged from the back room carrying boxes of jewelry to place in a display and unknowingly saved the moment from disaster.

"Come help me, would you, Cissy," Reta called out, then noticing Dub, she said, "Well hello, Dub. How're you doing? Bought all your school supplies yet?"

Dub stood to his full height and sauntered slowly to the jewelry counter. "Gosh no, Mrs. Hankins. You know I never get my stuff till the first day of school. What would the guys think if I had my things ahead of time like I was anxious and ready for school or something. They'd laugh theirselves silly at me."

Reta draped gold chains in the display case. She stopped to look up at Dub and laugh. "Oh, most certainly, Dub, we wouldn't want anyone to think you were eager for school to start, would we? But aren't you? I mean not even for football season?"

The cowboy awkwardly shifted his weight from one leg to the other, looking down at the scuffed toe of his boot. "Well now, Mrs. Hankins, when you put it that way…" He ran his fingers through his hair revealing the forehead which having been constantly shaded by his cowboy hat was paler than his ruddy cheeks. "I guess you could say I'm ready for football season to begin. And I'm more than ready for haying season to be over." He grinned. "I guess I'm a little more ready for school than I thought." He leaned a little closer to the glass counter. "You sure got a way of making a person speak the truth of a matter, Mrs. Hankins."

Although Dub had been taken off balance momentarily, he quickly regained his composure. "You sure do look fine and purty today, Mrs. Hankins. You could sure enough pass for the twins' sister, and that's a fact."

"Why, thank you, Dub," Reta said without looking up from her work, but Marcy knew her mother was trying not to laugh.

"Well, I best get back before chore time or Dad'll send a search party after me." He waved toward the soda fountain. "You girls keep up the good work on the cheering. You're gonna need it. And Mrs. Hankins, keep back my set of school supplies. I'll stop by first day of school and pick 'em up. Okay?"

"How about if I put them in the window display with a big old sign indicating whose they are?" Now Reta laughed out loud at the thought.

Dub threw up his hands in mock horror as he back out the door. "Whoo-ee! Don't be doing that. You'll ruin me for sure."

As his pickup roared down Main Street a few minutes later, Cissy said, "That phony loudmouth. Somebody needs to cut him down to size."

"Why Cissy Hankins," their mother said. "What a thing to say. I thought you liked Dub. He's such a fine, hard-working young man."

"That was before I realized how self-centered he is. He acts like he'd the only player on the team. How can he be so callous?"

Marcy, however, had regarded the young rancher with interest realizing for the first time how he contradicted himself. While outwardly he portrayed a cocky, sure attitude, at the same time, he felt threatened. She'd felt that way herself many times. Feeling threatened to the point that she must hurl out empty words to cover her feelings. Or retreat into a shell of silence.

"I can understand his being overwhelmed by Spence Caldwell," she said. "I guess I'd feel the same way if I were in his shoes. He doesn't quite know how to handle the situation. He's no longer tall hog at the trough."

"So that's how it is." Reta looked at both girls. "Did Dub say something about Spence before I came in?"

"Said we didn't need him," Cissy replied hotly. "Can you believe that? Our little team not needing a state champion? Can you think of anything more absurd?" Her chin was trembling.

"Marcy's right," their mother agreed. "Dub will need time to get used to the idea of having someone on the team that's his own size."

"Bigger," Cissy corrected. "A lot bigger."

"Not *that* much," Marcy retorted, and then wondered what she was doing in the middle of this silly conversation. She certainly didn't like Dub. Never had. So what did it matter?

Now Cissy's hands were on her hips. "Marcy, Spence is bigger and better in every way than Dub Weston ever thought about being. And that blowhard better not do anything to hinder Spence's playing out on that field, or he'll hear it from me."

"Stop fussing," Reta told them firmly. "I still feel it's important to help Dub by letting him know we support him as a player and as a person. Now let's get back to work."

"Support, my foot." Cissy wasn't convinced, even by her mother's reprimand. "Dub's got all the support he needs. From himself. He's the one who should be giving support to the newcomer. And that's Spence. Dub is acting like a little child." She tossed her head as she walked off. "And I now detest him."

Chapter Eleven

On the first day of school, the halls of Andonburg High School reverberated with voices, laughter, and slamming of locker doors as students filled the hallways. Marcy was her twin's carbon copy dressed in their red polo shirts and navy slacks. They twinned up according to Cissy's plan.

Not many things in nature used the brash color of red, Marcy thought to herself as she arranged books in her locker, except maybe a cardinal. Or a tulip. She didn't relish being a tulip; she had no interest in attracting honeybees.

"If I don't see you at lunch," Cissy was saying as she prepared to depart for her first class, "I'll see you at tryouts."

Tryouts. Marcy had been trying to forget. Her stomach tightened at the mere mention of the word. "Okay. See you there."

Cissy's reasoning in wearing red was no doubt because of the tryouts. Marcy would never have thought to wear red to attract the judges' attention. Perhaps they were the honeybees she would be attracting today.

Audrey Epperling was waiting for her at the door of the science room. "Hi," she said, greeting Marcy with a warm smile. "I saw on the schedule that we had Anatomy and Physiology together, so I thought I'd wait on you."

Audrey was a rather plain-looking, but very pleasant girl, who seemed content with her appearance, failing even to apply a hint of blush to her light complexioned cheeks. Marcy, however, was ready for Audrey's quiet company, since she accepted Marcy *as is*, demanding nothing.

"Thanks, Audrey. So good to see you. You think this will be a hard class?"

"For you? Nope."

"Hey, just because I did okay in biology last year doesn't mean this will be snap. Mr. Radford is no slouch, you know."

"Yeah, but he is rather taken with you because of all that entomology work you do. Everyone knows that."

At least Audrey didn't say *bugs*. Marcy gave a smile. "Good to know someone appreciates it."

Occasionally in the past, Audrey had served as a sounding board for Marcy's grieving about the lack of understanding toward her work. While Audrey had no love of insects either, she never hopped on the condemnation bandwagon.

Stepping into the science room, Marcy was faced with a double reaction. There in a seat by the windows sat Spence who raised his eyebrows in recognition, then opened his mouth to speak. At almost the same moment, Mr. Radford spoke.

"Hello Marcy. Good to have you back as one of my students."

The stocky, fortyish teacher had endeared himself to Marcy the previous year as he encouraged her to pursue a career in entomology. Now she quietly thanked him and prayed silently that he would say nothing about it in front of Spence. But how long could that go on? Sooner or later, it was bound to come out in the open.

How could such silly thoughts be going on in her mind? Why should she even care? Yet, she was grateful that Mr. Radford's only remark before the bell was to ask if she'd thought of any ideas for this year's science fair. She shook her head and took her seat.

Truthfully, her head had been swimming with several great ideas, which a few weeks ago, she'd been bursting to share with Mr. Radford. But now...

If the bell had been delayed, Marcy wondered what she would have done. Would she have turned to Spence and politely acknowledged him? Would she have introduced Audrey? Much as she hated to admit it, she wouldn't have known what to do.

Mr. Radford set about handing out the class syllabus, from which Marcy could see the class was going to be a real challenge. They were required to assemble the skeleton of a small animal, such as a rabbit or squirrel. In addition, two major research papers were due before the semester was out, and there appeared to be a considerable amount of homework outside the classroom. She knew this class would be an important grade on her transcript when she entered State in two years. At times, she loathed her small school and the limitations she faced in opportunities to study advanced sciences.

She heard Audrey whisper. "You're scowling. It can't be that bad."

Marcy shrugged, smiled, and tried to relax. As she did, she caught Spence's eye. Had he been looking at her before? He flashed his dimpled smile and she felt her cheeks redden. Audrey quickly looked over to the window to see who had caused her friend to blush. She then looked back at Marcy with a questioning look.

Marcy busied herself with the syllabus and tried not to look at anyone. She had to admit Spence was nice looking. Not terrific or any of the silly things Cissy said. Just very nice. Couldn't *nice* be an adequate word? To her it said a lot.

After class, as she and Audrey walked down the hall comparing their schedules, a voice called behind them. "Marcy, wait up." It was Spence.

"No sword fighting today?" he said as she turned around. "But still lots of red, right?"

"Right." It surprised her that he could call her out in the crowd, and that he would make reference to the silliness he witnessed in the alley. "We hammered our swords into Bic Fine Points for the duration," she retorted wielding the pen as she had the paint brush.

When he laughed at her joke, it caught her off guard. Others were now staring. "We haven't much time for class changes," she said. "We have to hurry. Good to see you again. Hope you like it here."

"Wait a minute." He pulled out his folded schedule. "I stopped you to ask where 132B is located. This may be a small school, but I'm already lost."

"You're headed in the right direction, but you're in the wrong building. All the B rooms are in the annex. Take a left at the end of this hall and you'll come right to it."

"Thanks." He waved the paper at her as he hurried on his way. "If you slay any dragons, let me know."

"I will." Her last words were barely a whisper. She scooted on her way to catch up with Audrey who had conveniently slipped off down the hall without her.

"Well, well." Audrey's voice was sing-song. "You forgot to tell me you were acquainted with Mr. Everybody's-Dream. Want to tell me about it?" Her voice indicated interest, but not too impressed. In her quiet way, Audrey wasn't all that excitable. It was a quality that Marcy liked.

"There's not much to tell. It was a chance meeting when he stopped by the drug store looking for empty boxes. Cissy and I were painting the old desk that's now sitting in the window. We were acting crazy when he came. It was terribly embarrassing." Once again, she avoided saying anything about the original meeting at Kendallwood. The story was too complicated; it was best to keep the facts simple.

"I bet every girl in Andonburg High wishes their father owned the drug store then," Audrey commented dryly.

Marcy felt she needed to add, "Cissy is really taken with him."

"She would be. Does Dub know?"

Marcy marveled at her friend's perception. "No. And he's already bad-mouthed Spence in Cissy's presence which set the sparks smoldering."

"I can imagine. Are you the referee?"

Marcy sighed. She wanted to say, "I'm the referee and the margin of safety," but instead she just said, "I hope not," and let it go at that.

As they entered the English classroom, Marcy now wished she'd glanced at Spence's schedule to see if they had any other classes together. Since he was a senior, it wasn't likely. She put her hand to her throat and pressed hard to stop the pulsating that bounced up from her heart, while firmly telling herself that he had stopped her only to ask directions. Nothing more.

At lunch, Marcy headed to the table where she saw Cissy and Winnie sitting, dragging Audrey in her wake. Cissy, however, was up and gone the moment she saw Selena Thomas appear in the cafeteria. She seemed to be asking the senior several questions which demanded immediate answers.

Marcy couldn't imagine what could be so important to talk about at this late date. Tryouts were now only a few hours away.

Picking at the salad on her plate, Winnie said, "You ready for the big moment, Shorty?"

"As ready as I'll ever be, Coach," Marcy shot back.

"Ready?" Audrey wanted to know. "Ready for what?"

"Haven't you heard?" Winnie said. "Marcy's trying out for cheerleader this year."

"Marcy?" Audrey gave her a surprised look. "Whatever for?"

It was the kind of question only Audrey could have asked. Audrey, who knew and appreciated how involved Marcy was with her work, and how content she'd always been with it.

"Well," Marcy started, hating already that her tone sounded apologetic. "Cissy's been talking about..." She stopped and started again. "Actually, I decided to be involved in a few more extracurricular activities this year. It looks good on a transcript. Colleges look at those things, you know."

"Your entomology work is an extracurricular activity." Audrey's clear green eyes were still looking straight at her. It was a bit irritating. First Cissy, then her mother, and now Audrey. Everyone seemed to think they knew what was best for her. How was she ever going to find out for herself?

"The decision has already been made, Audrey," she said. "If I make it in the tryouts, I'll be on the varsity squad this fall. And I think it's going to be fun," she added defensively, if not thoroughly convincing.

Chapter Twelve

Every girl who showed up for tryouts was nervous and giggly as they lined up on the stage in the school auditorium. First, they would face a team of private judges brought in from outside the community. This year, those judges were cheerleaders from the nearby state college who had agreed to come and help out.

Following the private tryouts, the student body could vote after various routines were presented on stage in the all-school assembly. The students' votes were combined with the judges' scores to reveal the outcome. The results were to be posted the following day.

The hours of practice that Winnie and Cissy forced on Marcy paid off. When it came time for her solo routine in front of the judges, in spite of the fact that her nerves were rattled, she executed each one smooth and easy. When it was over she felt as though she were back in junior high, with that all-bubbly sensation. She almost felt like another person altogether.

On stage, performing before the entire student body, she, Winnie, and Cissy performed two of their more complicated routines. Marcy could distinctly hear Dub yelling and giving shrill whistles after they'd finished. Dub made no secret of his infatuation over Cissy. The entire school knew.

When they arrived at school the next morning, Marcy said to her twin, "You go look at the results. I'd rather hear it from you." She stood outside the school office and waited. When she saw Cissy's pale, drawn face as she came out it was obvious something had gone wrong.

She took hold of Cissy's arm. "What is it? Are we in?"

"Maureen," she muttered shaking her head. "Maureen is head cheerleader over us. Selena is the other one, and they placed Winnie on junior varsity squad." Her last words made it sound like a fate worse than death.

Marcy had thought from the outset that it was wrong of Cissy to intentionally try to shut Maureen out, but instead of saying so, instead of standing her ground, she'd joined in the scheme. Now she was in and Winnie, who had worked so hard with them, was the one who was shut out. Marcy could see the hurt in Cissy's eyes, and even thought it was her sister's own fault, she slipped her arm around Cissy's shoulders to console her.

"It was tough competition, Cissy. Even a spot with junior varsity is a privilege."

Cissy shook her head in disbelief. "How could they have chosen Maureen over Winnie? And how are we going to tell her?"

At that moment, Marcy saw Winnie's bright red hair through the crowded hallway. As she approached, her eyes were red-rimmed from crying, but her smile was bright as ever. Marcy knew instantly that Winnie already knew the results, had gone off to cry alone and was ready to bounce back. It was no wonder that everyone in the school loved Winnie Denton.

"Hail to the varsity cheerleaders," she called out.

Cissy looked as if she were about to faint. "Winnie, I'm so sorry..."

But Winnie wouldn't let her finish. "Sorry nothing. Everything was fair and square, and you two did splendidly." She gave Marcy a big hug. "Especially you. I can't believe it. You were absolutely terrific."

Marcy received the hug and the praises, although she felt she deserved neither one. She was now a cheerleader, primarily because of Cissy's silly scheme that had backfired. Had she not caved in, Winnie might now be a varsity cheerleader with Cissy. The place where both had wanted to be from the beginning.

A pep rally was set for third hour in the gym to announce the results, as though word had not spread throughout the school like wildfire. With great finesse, Maureen led her new team through the routines and the gymnasium vibrated with the resounding cheers of the student body.

Standing before the entire school as their elected representative, Marcy suddenly felt incredibly stiff and wooden. Now she was destined to stand before all those eyes for the remainder of the season.

Cissy had no such qualms. Her face beamed with pure delight and every part of her body seemed alive and vibrant. It occurred to Marcy to wonder if she would have ever been elected had it not been for *twinning up*. To someone else, the response might be *who cares*. But for Marcy it was a sticky question that she couldn't shake.

That evening at supper, the Hankins family heard every detail from Cissy's excited play-by-play of the day. When their mother voiced her concern that Winnie might have been hurt over the results, Cissy assured her that Winnie was such a good sport that it didn't bother her a bit being on junior squad, just so she was a cheerleader.

Marcy was appalled at Cissy's lack of concern for Winnie. Of course, that was what Winnie said, but it was only a front. How she wished Cissy would be honest enough to admit that Winnie had been hurt. Forgiving yes, but still hurt. But Cissy was moving on to other important matters.

"And you'll never guess what else," she was saying between bites of pork chops. "Remember how excited Maureen was to have Spence at her house for their little barbeque? Well, I asked her today how the party turned out and what she thought of Spence. And what do you know." Her voice went higher with each word. "His aunt and uncle came, but Spence didn't even show." She laughed aloud. "So, I got to meet him first after all."

"And what difference does that make?" her father wanted to know.

Cissy gave a snort of disbelief. "Why, Daddy, it gives me a head start. Sort of an *in* with Spence that Maureen doesn't have."

Alan shook his head. "Cissy, you met the guy for a minute when he picked up boxes. How can you be so sure you even want to know him any better?"

"I just know, that's all. I think it's important in life to size up a situation and move into action right away. That's how you get to be where you want to be."

Yeah. Like attempting to shove Maureen out of her cheerleading spot, Marcy wanted to say. Instead she held her peace.

"I know right now," Cissy went on, "that Spence is simply too wonderful for words. Just a perfect type of guy. So handsome, kind, and thoughtful..."

"Ugh!" Bernie said twisting his face into a horrid scowl. "Dad, make her stop. She's ruining my appetite talking so mushy about a star football player like that."

"Quiet, Peanut. This isn't your concern."

"My stomach's my concern."

As they squabbled, Marcy was thinking how trite Cissy made it all sound. She was sure that if she ever had a special someone, she would ponder it all in her heart and not broadcast it around the dinner table for all to hear.

"By the way, Marcy," Cissy broke into her thoughts. "We're meeting tomorrow night at Maureen's to vote on our uniforms. Then we'll be planning fund-raising projects to go toward the uniform expenses." She pushed her chair away from the table. "Now if I can be excused, I've got to call Winnie and see if she has our history assignment. Wish you were in that class with us, Marcy. Then I could just get it from you."

So, it was beginning already. Marcy shuddered. The stepped-up pace of the active life of a cheerleader.

For better or for worse, she was in.

Chapter Thirteen

T he outcome of the first cheerleaders' meeting wasn't too pleasing in Marcy's opinion. They met at Maureen's house with both squads present, along with the young Miss Santeen, the new PE teacher and their sponsor, who had not yet learned the girls' personalities. Had she known, she would have put a lid on Maureen's efforts to run the whole show.

Maureen's mother moved graciously in and out of their spacious, wood-paneled den checking to make sure everyone had adequate refills of sodas, chips, and sandwiches.

As the meeting got under way, Maureen remained standing, evidently in order to remain in charge. At one point she was holding up a sewing pattern package that pictured a puff-sleeved blouse on the front, a blouse that she was convinced would become part of their uniform.

"We can buy matching skirts and vests and sew our own blouses," she explained waving the pattern, "which will make it *so* much more economical for each one of us."

Having entered the room at that minute with a fresh tray of sandwiches, her mother heard the remark and exclaimed in her Southern drawl as thick as

Maureen's, "Why Maureen, what a thoughtful suggestion. A splendid way for the girls to save money."

Sitting off by herself at the end of a long couch, Marcy did a slow burn. They made it sound as if all the other girls were paupers. It amazed her how everyone seemed bent on pleasing Maureen. Even Cissy had chosen this moment to don her more docile personality. Probably in repentance for the foul-up in the elections.

How she wished she had the courage to stand up and tell them that if they were going to have fund raisers for uniforms, what difference could it make? Sewing or buying, the difference would be miniscule. Add to that the fact that everyone knew neither Maureen nor her mother could sew a stitch, and they would send hers out to be made by someone else. And last but not least, who among them, with their busy school schedules, had a moment to spare to sew a blouse?

She must have been scowling because Cissy sent her a questioning glance from across the room. Marcy ignored her.

Meanwhile, Miss Santeen seemed to be gung-ho on the idea as well. "You'll appreciate them more if you put something of yourselves into them," she said in her college-fresh young voice.

Marcy wanted to gag. *I'll appreciate my blouse if I can buy the thing and have my precious time back.*

On the way home, Cissy reminded her that to be a cheerleader, she needed to have a little bit of cheer. That verbal slam was almost too much. Usually it was the other way around. Her cheering up Cissy.

.⁺.₊ ° ♡ °.₊⁺.

On Monday evening, Marcy had every intention of slipping out of the house after finishing sewing the sleeves into the bodice of her cheerleading blouse. The puff sleeves with so much extra fabric were tricky to gather and stitch.

Just as she was finished and ready to leave the house, Cissy was holding her own blouse and moaning that she just couldn't get the sleeves pinned in right in order to sew them in. She'd already had to rip out the stitching in the cuffs and redo them once. Cissy was just too impatient to take the time to do it right.

"Can you help me please, Marcy? There's so much material here, it keeps getting away from me."

All too soon the evening was spent. She was sure she could get to her workroom the next evening and she tumbled into bed exhausted.

The remainder of the week flew by as she was pressed in from all sides with various meetings and activities, plus all the homework that reared its ugly head—most particularly in anatomy class. In the midst of it all Marcy managed to squeeze in two brief stints of working with her entomology, but they were entirely inadequate.

A car wash was slated for the following Saturday as their first fundraiser. Their parents agreed to allow them to get off work at two in the afternoon to go help.

During the morning hours at the store on Saturday, Marcy's mind was constantly on her projects. Somehow, she had to find a way to get back there and catch up.

In a quiet moment, she approached her mother and asked if she could skip lunch and spend that hour in her workroom.

Reta eyed her daughter. "You have been rather busy lately, haven't you?"

Remembering her mother's earlier admonition, Marcy quickly went on the defense. "Not *too* busy. It's just that I have a few unfinished details that need attention right away. How about it?"

"This time," her mother said as she went back to arranging the cosmetic display. "But promise not to make this a habit. That work is to be done in the evenings, not during your work days."

"Promise. And thanks."

At precisely twelve, she slipped away and feverishly began making systematic checks. Her worse fears were realized as she discovered two of her prize larvae were dead. Disgusted, she dumped them in the trash. She scolded herself for the waste, remembering the time and effort it took to collect them in the first place.

Hurriedly she labeled the remaining aquatic insects, scouring her books for their scientific names. One had her stumped, but eventually she found it and made out that label as well.

Both display cases were still weak in her opinion. Frustration and confusion sparred around in her head. She rubbed the back of her aching neck. Was it right that she allowed a few bugs to make her this upset?

Bugs? Had that word actually entered into her head? Whatever was the matter with her?

The door to the workroom opened and her mother stood there looking at her sternly. "Marcy, I can't believe you would abuse your privileges this way."

"Abuse? What do you mean?"

"You've been here for almost an hour and a half."

Marcy felt her heart sink. It'd seemed like only a few minutes. She still had so much to do. Two butterflies yet to be lifted from their spreading blocks, mounted, and labeled.

"I'm so sorry," she said softly. "I guess I just lost all track of time."

"That thing on your wrist is call a watch. You're supposed to watch it. Remember? Now come on back to work because we're snowed under."

Closing the door on her workroom, she felt her shame changing into resentment as she thought of all the times Cissy and Bernie goofed off without ever being caught. But now she'd spent a few extra minutes with her work and she was in trouble. Of course, she knew a half hour was more than a *few minutes,* but still it just wasn't fair.

Later, her father told her she could make up the extra thirty minutes by working until two-thirty rather than getting off early as planned. Missing part of the car wash was no bother to Marcy, but Cissy disagreed vehemently.

"What do you mean you're coming later?" her sister asked sharply when Marcy told her to go on without her.

"Dad says I have to make up the thirty minutes I spent in my workroom during lunch."

"Marcy, we must show up together. You're one of the team now. You've got a responsibility to the office you hold. Why'd you have to go and spoil everything with your old bugs?"

"Spoil everything? Excuse me, but thirty minutes will *not* spoil anything."

"And how will it look to Maureen if we're not on time? We've got a certain reputation to uphold you know." Then with an air of adult self-assuredness, she added, "Well never mind. It'll be okay this time. I'm going to wait on you and if we get into trouble, it will be together."

Marcy turned away to wait on a customer. It was more than she could stomach.

.⁺·₊ ° ♡ °₊·⁺.

The first football game was on the home field and the night was a perfect fall evening with just enough chill in the air to smell crisp and sharp. The ebony sky was clear and filled with sparkling stars. Marcy could sense the electrifying excitement as they walked from their house to the field, which was laid out on a solitary level space a few blocks from the high school building.

Through the trees the field lights appeared to light up that end of town in a soft hazy glow. Marcy wished she'd grabbed her heavy coat instead of the sweater she had with her. Of course, later she'd be on the field with no wrap on at all, but it would have been nice to have it for half time break. By the time the game got underway, she forgot all about being cold and was absorbed in the thrill of the game.

Spence, as it turned out, truly was the star of the game. Marcy watched in amazement as he intercepted passes and made touchdown after touchdown. Andonburg fans were going crazy.

Football was big in Andonburg. The whole town turned out for home games, whether or not they had students involved. Many of the old-timers re-lived their own glory days on that field as they now cheered for the younger players.

"That Caldwell kid runs like the wind," Marcy overheard a gray-haired guy commenting as she stood in line at the refreshment stand for a cup of steaming hot chocolate. "Wouldn't old man Kendallwood have been bustin' his buttons to think his kin would lead our guys to victory?"

Right away, Marcy sensed the significance attached to the fact that Spence, however remotely, had his roots on this little town. As such, he wasn't really an outsider.

Her own father has spent many years winning over Andonburg's townsfolk since he hailed from Chicago. Few felt he could be trusted since he was a full-fledged Yankee.

Shortly after halftime, once the game was under way again, a sleek black limousine pulled up and parked directly behind the Andonburg bleachers. Two men in business suits stepped out of the car. A black limo was nearly as rare a sight in Andonburg as a candy-apple red Corvette.

Marcy hadn't seen the car herself, but Audrey, who played clarinet in the pep band was right there on the bleachers and saw it all, then filled Marcy in on the details later.

She did, however, see a large man pushing his way through the crowd to press in at the edge of the playing field. Almost immediately, twittering spread through the crowd like wind in a ripe wheat field. It was, they said, none other than Spence's own father.

Not content on the sidelines, the man stepped right up to Coach York and shook his hand. Marcy detected no warmness in Mr. Caldwell's expression. In fact, from where the cheerleaders were standing, they could hear his brusque voice which bordered on being harsh.

When Coach York asked him to step back out of the way, Spence's father let Coach know he could very well stand wherever he pleased.

"Stand where you please," Coach's answer came back, "but don't bother me during the game. I've got a job to do."

The second man now stepped up to the duo and laid a hand on Mr. Caldwell's shoulder as though to encourage him to move out of the way. Mr. Caldwell, however, did not budge.

Marcy was now very curious. She wondered if Spence knew that his father had come to watch him play. She could scarcely keep her mind on the cheers for watching the impervious man with slightly graying hair and craggy brows. Once the game again grew so exciting that no one had a mind for anything else, Marcy watched him quietly vanish from the scene.

Spence had been on the field the entire time.

14

Chapter Fourteen

According to tradition, the Hankins opened the malt shop for an hour or so following the victorious game. Soon the kids were crowded into the booths, clustered about the glass-topped tables, and overflowed the counter stools.

Marcy and Cissy were corralled into working without a minute to catch a breath. Even Winnie was called into action helping take orders and relay them to the Hankins behind the counter. Soon aromas of hamburgers and fries filled the store along with the super-charged excitement from the win.

Presently, Spence walked in and sat down with a couple of the team players at one of the tables. Most of the players, however, were at the counter where Dub sat with his buddy, Carson Cates.

Now, added to Spence's already alluring appeal was the mystery of his forceful father, and the proof of his amazing skills on the football field. Not a girl in the room could keep from watching him. That included including Maureen Ratherfield.

Cissy's mind wasn't idle either. She insisted on slipping out from behind the counter to wait on Spence's table herself. As she did so, she whispered to Marcy. "Maureen won't have an excuse like mine. Watch this!"

Marcy watched.

"You did great out there, tonight, Spence," Cissy said as she stepped to where Spence sat. "I can't believe your speed. Can I get you anything?"

Just then, Dub turned around. "Hey, Cissy," he said in his too-loud voice. "It took a lot of blocking and tackling to get that guy down the field tonight."

Cissy gave Dub a sour look and told him to hush.

"Marcy," Winnie said, "you're overflowing a Coke cup."

"Oops. Thanks, Winnie. Wasn't watching."

"I know. Interesting, isn't it?"

Marcy couldn't hear the rest of what was said, but Cissy was soon back at the grill saying to her father, "Spence wants a hamburger, Dad. I'll fix it for him."

Alan stepped aside with an exaggerated bow. "Be my guest, Chef. And you can cook all the rest of them as well. Four orders are ahead of the star player's." And to show he meant it, he stepped aside to starting putting fries in waiting baskets.

At first, Cissy was disarmed, but rallied quickly and whipped out the orders, then turned her attention to the one for Spence. Unnoticed by Alan, she tucked in a bonus of fries in the basket with the burger. As she stepped out to deliver the order, a hand caught her arm.

"Say now," Dub said. "I didn't hear him order no fries. How come he's the only one who gets freebies around here?"

"Let go of me, Dub Weston. I've got work to do."

"Whoever could this be for?" he asked in a mocking tone, as he gazed around the room. Then he looked at his buddies and grinned. "As if we didn't know, right?"

A ripple of laughter now egged him on.

"Must be for the fleet-footed, twinkle-toes."

"Dub, stop acting like a child. Let me go before you make me drop this."

"Tut, tut. Such a tragedy that would be." More laughter.

Marcy was about ready to jump out and stop the nonsense, but her father was a step ahead of her.

"Problems?" he said to Dub.

"Gee, Mr. Hankins," he said making his voice a high whine. "It don't seem quite fair for Cissy to give free fries to Mr. Corvette over there when all of us only get a few chips with ours. All of us worked hard to get that guy down the field tonight. Don't we get a break?"

"You order fries, you get fries," Alan told him. "If not, you get chips."

"Unless your name is Spence Caldwell," Dub countered. "He gets fries when he doesn't order 'em."

Spence who had sized up the situation spoke up. "No problem. I did want the fries, and I'll be more than happy to pay for them. I didn't realize how hungry I really was."

His unaffected manner seemed to let everyone know that none of this banter bothered him. Marcy was impressed.

"Marcy," her mother said, pointing. She was letting another Coke cup run over.

But Dub wasn't finished. "Say, I got an idea. Why don't Mr. Corvette over there, whose daddy comes wheeling up in his Batmobile to tell Coach York how to run the game, buy us all a round of fries. Since he's got it, we'll let him flaunt it."

Alan quieted the whoops of laughter and instructed Dub to can it or leave. Then he settled everything by offering free fries to every team member. Turning to Cissy, he lifted the precious basket from her hands. "I'll take this and you serve up the fries since you were so anxious to help."

At the grill again, Cissy did a slow boil. "Can you believe that Dub Weston? He's nothing but a spoiled brat," she fumed.

"Cissy," Marcy said softly, "you know it's our policy not to give favors to one and not to another." Secretly, Marcy was glad her sister's manipulations had failed.

"Oh pooh on policy. I was only trying to show my appreciation to our star player."

"In case you missed it, there was a team out on that field, Cissy."

"Maybe so," Cissy said as she filled another basket with steaming fries, "but we sure didn't beat Pinedale last year with the team we had."

✦⁺·₊ ° ♡ °₊ ·⁺✦

When the magic moment finally arrived, the moment when Marcy could place her head on her pillow that night, as exhausted as she was, she was sure sleep would fall on her like a warm fuzzy blanket. However, she hadn't counted on a play-by-play of the drama of the evening by her sister.

At the end of her tirade she said, "I was only trying to do something nice, and Dad took Dub's side and made me look like a fool in front of everyone," she moaned. "I'll never live it down."

One would have thought the sheer agony of it all would have kept Cissy awake for hours, but within minutes of her final sentence, her even breathing told Marcy that her effervescent sister had finally lost her fizz.

It was in that moment, as she now tried to get to sleep herself, that she suddenly realized that the Ambrose County Fair's opening day was next Thursday. She sat straight up in bed. Next Thursday! That meant exhibits must be taken to Beltonville fairgrounds on Wednesday evening.

Methodically, her mind listed last minute work to be done. Silently she slipped out of bed and padded across the carpet to her desk. After switching on the desk lamp, she scratched a few notes on her notepad. Crawling back into bed, she vowed at least one evening next week would be devoted to her workroom.

That time finally became available on Tuesday night, by which time she was nearly in a panic. Even then, Cissy was begging for help with her Algebra. Firmly, Marcy refused. "Call Winnie. I've got to go to the store and get my cases ready for the fair tomorrow."

"The fair? Already?"

"Already. And my cases will have to be entered by five o'clock."

"Oh, your cases are all okay. They'll get blue ribbons just like last year. There's nobody in the county that's much competition for you."

"I wouldn't say that. Wesley Pennington is highly creative and his club is building a strong entomology group." Inwardly, Marcy wondered how he could find interested kids when everyone in Andonburg laughed at her.

Perhaps she should give talks to some of the grade school science classes and drum up some interest that way. Why hadn't she thought of that before? Then in a few years her own club would have a group of entomologists as well.

"Wesley," Cissy said into the silence. "He's a nice guy, isn't he?"

"So, so." She gave a noncommittal wave. "Gotta run. Hope Winnie can help out with the algebra."

As she went out the door, Cissy was still talking. "On Friday night we'll drive over and see what you got on the exhibits and take in the midway."

"Okay. Whatever."

The evening was warm as she stepped quickly in the direction of Main Street. Indian summer had slipped in and chased the fall coolness away. She was anxious to get back into her workroom, where she felt the most comfortable. In the privacy of her workroom, she set about lifting butterflies from the spreading blocks and mounting them with insect pins in her display case, and then labeled each one. Feeding the larvae, she noticed one had begun to spin its cocoon. She made notes in her log book. The book that had once boasted a steady stream of notes now looked rather sporadic.

A sharp rap at the front door of the store startled her. Certainly, no Andonburg resident would come knocking at this time of night. If there was an emergency, Alan was called at the house.

Her heart pounding, she slipped out of her room and tiptoed across the storage area to the door that led into the main part of the store. She'd often heard horror stories of drug addicts who came to rob small-town drug stores of their narcotics. But surely a thief wouldn't be polite enough to knock.

Peering from the backroom across the expanse of the store, Darcy could see Spence Caldwell peering back at her through cupped hands against the front door glass.

15

Chapter Fifteen

At first Marcy snickered out loud at the sight of the face pressed against the glass, but then she noticed his expression of concern.

"Marcy," he said when she opened the door, "I'm so glad you're here."

"Come in, Spence. What's your problem?"

"It's Uncle Fred. He needs his prescription filled and for some reason our phone's not working."

"Welcome to small-town America. It includes bad phone service."

"I saw the emergency number on the door and was about to go use a pay phone when I saw the light in the back. I'm not bothering you, am I?"

"Bother? Heavens no. Come on over to the counter and sit down. I'll call Dad. He'll be here in a jiffy. Is it an emergency?"

"Not an 'in a minute' emergency, but certainly a 'by in the morning' emergency." He seated himself at the counter.

After she'd hung up from calling home, Marcy said, "Do you want something to drink while you're waiting?"

Spence had been surveying the store and now he spun back around on the bar stool. "Drink? Well, now. Are you the soda jerk?" Then he added quickly, "Not that you're a jerk." Then he laughed.

She let her laughter join with his. "I'm the jerk," she agreed. In more ways than she cared to admit. "What'll it be?"

"Do you make limeades with fizz water or with Sprite?"

"No fakes at the Hankins' Malt Shop. We deal in the genuine article." She exaggerated the words to make it sound like a corny television commercial.

"That's for me," he said. "The kids love this place, don't they?"

"Some do. Syrup heavy or easy?"

"Heavy." He was looking around again. "It looks like the fifties malt shops you see depicted in the movies."

Marcy wasn't sure what to say. To her their store was modern and up-to-date. Then she realized it must be the smallness that appealed to him.

"So, what keeps you in the store so late?" he asked. "Slave labor?"

"Just some work of my own," she hedged, setting the frosty glass down in front of him. With quick thinking she changed the subject. "Is Andonburg much different than what you're used to?"

"Much," he said. Then took a long sip of his limeade. "Big cities are such a rat race."

"But there are advantages of a larger city, right?"

"Such as?"

"Anonymity."

"That could also be known as getting lost in the masses."

"But the opposite is to have everything known about everyone. Pre-judged and pressed into some sort of mold that impossible to escape from."

It must have been the emotion she put into her words that caused Spence to study her face till she felt it growing warm. Finally, he took another drink. "I suppose there's good and bad about both."

"You'll have a hard time getting a football scholarship living here."

He smiled. "That shouldn't worry you, since you won't be needing one."

"No, but I do need advanced science courses that larger schools provide. Sometimes I feel like I'm getting cheated."

"The limeade is terrific," he said lifting the glass toward her. "What will your college major be if you need all that science stuff?"

The word "entomology" was on the tip of her tongue when her father came through the front door and the question was forgotten. He quickly set about filling the prescription from the paper Spence handed him, asking all the while about the team and the football season.

When Spence had given them a polite thank-you and good-bye, her father offered her a ride home. Only after she was seated beside him in the car did she fully realize what had just happened. She had had a casual conversation with Spence Caldwell. She had not been nervous, ill at ease, nor did she put her foot in her mouth. It was a miracle. She couldn't help but wonder what Cissy would say when she found out. Marcy cringed to think about it.

As they pulled in their driveway, her father turned and said, "Cissy's pretty crazy about that guy isn't she."

"Yeah she is." No denying it, *crazy* was putting it mildly.

"Do you think it best then if we didn't mention who appeared at the store tonight? That is, unless she presses the subject."

Marcy gave a heavy sigh. "That'd be great, Dad. Thanks so much." His understanding took her a little off guard.

Wednesday after school, as she loaded her insect cases into the car to go to Beltonville, she was almost despondent. Angry for cheating herself on time and effort that she should have invested in the exhibits.

Driving out of town she passed the Kendallwood estate and gazed longingly at the house and grounds. She slowed the car to see if she could detect any major changes. None were apparent other than flowers blooming in the front around the portico.

It didn't take long to drop off the exhibits at the 4-H building. She had no desire to stick around and see what was going on at the midway. A purple Grand Champion ribbon hanging from each of her cases was all that she had on her mind.

.⁺. ° ♡ ° .⁺.

No football game was scheduled that Friday because nearly all of the Andonburg kids would pile into cars and drive to the Ambrose County Fair. When Marcy and Cissy drove into the parking lot of the dusty fairgrounds, Marcy asked her sister not to go with her to the exhibit hall. She preferred to receive the initial shock while alone.

Slowly she descended the steps into the cool recesses of the basement of the building. The old stone structure had stood there housing fair exhibits for several generations. She passed the elaborate floral exhibits, the oil paintings, and the ceramics. She held her breath as she approached the shelves of entomology cases. Her eyes scanned the cases. Then she spied them. Blue ribbons were fastened to each one, but the spectacular purple cluster ribbon fluttered from Wesley Pennington's.

"Sorry." The voice behind her startled her.

She turned to see Wesley standing there. He had a kind face. His slender build made him seem taller, but he was only a couple inches above her. He pushed his glasses up on his nose in a sort of nervous gesture.

"Don't be sorry." She was having a tough time finding her voice.

"But I know how badly you wanted it."

"Do you?"

He stepped toward her and put his hand gently on her shoulder. "So much so that I almost withdrew from the competition."

She forced a little laugh. "Oh Wesley, now that's just plain silly."

"Maybe. Maybe not."

"But thank you all the same."

"What say let's forget all about bugs for a while and take in the midway."

Bugs? Wesley had said *bugs*? Maybe he was more relaxed about his endeavors than she was. Not so defensive. It usually threw her into a tizzy when kids referred to her insects as bugs. Maybe she did need to loosen up.

"All right. Let's go."

"Marcy! Hello!"

She whirled around to see Spence standing there. What in the world was he doing in the basement of the exhibit hall? None of the kids she knew were interested in the exhibits shown in this area. They were all out on the midway.

"Spence. What a surprise."

"I could say the same thing." He walked toward them, his smile gleaming. "What brings you here?"

"Spence," she said evading the question, "I'd like you to meet a friend of mine, Wesley Pennington. Wesley, this is Spence Caldwell. He's new in Andonburg. A senior."

Wesley gave a firm handshake. "Glad to meet you, Spence. I saw you play in a game in Oklahoma City last year. I enjoy watching you play, man."

"Thanks for the compliment. You play for Beltonville?"

"Not me. I'm better in the bleachers. Say, Marcy and I were about to check out the midway. Care to come along? We could round up Cissy for a foursome. Right Marcy?"

Just standing next to Spence sent Marcy's heart pounding. How she wished she'd run into Spence when she was alone and he had asked her to be with him. But what could she say now? "Sure," she said. "Cissy won't be hard to find." *Especially when Spence is around.*

Indeed, Cissy wasn't hard to find at all. She'd seen Spence enter the exhibit hall and was hanging out at a nearby Sno-Cone booth waiting and watching.

"Hi Cissy," Wesley called out, who by this time has possessively taken Marcy's hand. At any other time she wouldn't have minded. She and Wesley had known one another since fifth grade. But now her heart was aching to be with Spence. She was being utterly ridiculous. She'd forgotten for a moment that every girl in Andonburg was after Spence. He had his pick.

Cissy moved slowly in their direction as though she just happened along at that moment. "Well, look who we have here," she said looking directly at Spence.

"We were about to head to the midway," Wesley said to her, even though Cissy hadn't even acknowledged his presence. "Want to come along?"

"Well, I don't know," she said taking a bite from her Sno-Cone, "am I wanted?"

It was all Marcy could do to keep from rolling her eyes. Just like Cissy to play drama queen.

"Sure you are," Spence said. "It ought to take all of five minutes to make the rounds of this massive midway."

Cissy hopped to his side without further encouragement.

"Hey now, Spence," Wesley said, "don't give us a complex about the size of our county fair. It's all we've got."

"Big or small the hucksters are just as obnoxious," Marcy said looking down the long row of brightly-lit booths. "The State Fair in Tulsa isn't much better. Just more to it." She was probably sounding like a killjoy, but fairs just weren't her thing. At least not the midway.

Cissy, on the other hand, was in her prime and was already begging Spence to take her on the octopus ride. He finally agreed, but Wesley and Marcy declined.

"I'm going to win Marcy a big old teddy bear to make up for whipping her again in her entomology entries," Wesley said.

"Entomology?" Spence looked at her.

Now it was out! Marcy felt hot all over in spite of the cool evening breeze. Now he would realize she was nothing but a Bug Brain. A girl that no one appreciated except a guy like Wesley Pennington.

Cissy picked up on the situation immediately. "Bugs! You know, creepy crawlies. Yuk. She messes with them all the time. Catches them, kills them, pins them. I don't see how she stands it. It's awful. Come on, Spence, the octopus ride stopped. We can ride now."

Good to his word, Wesley did win a teddy bear for her. Not a big one, but soft and cuddly. She chose the lavender one which would look perfect on the comforter on her bed. The sweet gesture from Wesley, however, did nothing to ease the devastation she felt inside now that Spence knew the truth.

When the four of them had regrouped and had finished off steaming corndogs, Marcy happened to notice Dub Weston striding forcefully toward them. He was flanked by his buddies, Carson Cates and Vic Moffitt.

Closing the gap between them, Dub called out, "Caldwell, what're you doing with my girl?"

Cissy stepped right up to Dub. "Since when did I become anyone's private property?"

Marcy watched Spence carefully. He was unruffled. "Had she told me she was taken, Dub, I wouldn't have even considered being with her. But the girl has a mind of her own. Why not let her decide?"

Dub stepped around Cissy and was nose-to-nose with Spence. In Marcy's opinion, he was making a perfect fool of himself.

"Please Dub," Marcy said, "You're making a scene. People are watching."

"You butt out, Professor Bug Brain. I don't need your mouth in this."

Now Wesley stepped forward. "That's a rude way to talk to a lady. Where're your manners?"

"Lady?" Dub sputtered. "Marcy?"

It was obvious Dub could have smashed Wesley with one hand tied behind his back, which made Marcy doubly proud of him for taking up for her.

But Dub would not be distracted. "Come on, Caldwell. Out back of the cattle barns. Let's settle this thing. I'll teach you to try to take my girl."

Spence smiled. "Well now, if you prefer the cattle barns, Dub, that's fine with me. We prefer the midway. Come on troupe," he said turning to leave.

It must have been the cool brush-off that caused Dub to explode. He stepped forward ready to swing. In one swift move Spence caught that arm, neatly whipped it behind Dub's back, catching him in a tight hold. Mercifully, Carson and Vic moved away when they realized their leader has been bested. Marcy considered it a miracle that they didn't all three plow into Spence.

Struggling to get free, Dub said, "Caldwell, I'll make you pay for this. Now let me go."

"I'll let go when you apologize to my friends here and when you make up your mind to leave us alone."

After more huffing and twisting, Dub did apologize and was set free. Walking away from them backward he shook his finger at Spence. "You think you can come barging in on us with your big city ways, Caldwell. You'll pay for this, I promise." His boots sent up puffs of dust as he stomped away, still flanked by his two buddies.

"I'm so sorry," Cissy was saying to Spence. "I had no idea... I mean I don't know how he ever thought..."

"Forget it. No harm done." Spence took Cissy's hand and the resumed their walk as though nothing had happened.

Later when it was time for the twins to leave, the guys walked them out to their car to say good-by. All the way home, Cissy kept up a line of chatter that was designed to drive Marcy absolutely insane.

"Oh Marcy, there's no way I can ever thank you enough for getting me together with Spence tonight. It was the most wonderful moment in my life. Ever. And I mean ever. I just wish Maureen could have seen me. Spence is *so* wonderful. *So* perfect. I can't even imagine any guy ever being more wonderful."

And on and on. The trouble was, Marcy agreed with every word. Why did it have to be that the only boy she'd ever been even remotely interested in, had to be one that her sister was batty over?

⋆⁺⋅₊ ° ♡ ° ₊⋅⁺⋆

On Monday morning as she was coming out of Mr. Radford's classroom, Spence stopped in the hall. "Marcy, you got a minute?"

She turned to meet the soft blueness of his eyes. Calming her voice she said, "Sure, Spence. What's up?"

"Pennington tells me that you used to come to the grounds at Kendallwood to search for insects. Is that right?"

Wesley? How in the world had they been talking on that subject? And when? And why? Marcy did remember telling Wesley about Kendallwood when she saw him at a 4-H judging school a while back.

She nodded. "I did. For a few months."

"Until we came?"

Now she was embarrassed. But she couldn't lie. "Yes."

"I'd like to invite you back whenever you want. I've talked it over with Uncle Fred and Aunt Daisy and they agree. You're welcome to use the grounds."

Marcy's breath was coming in short gasps. Could she be hearing right? The warning buzzer sounded for next class. "I want to, but I don't want to intrude."

"No intrusion." He shrugged his shoulders. "Like I said, we've talked it over. You're welcome. Anytime. Just give us a call." He chuckled. "The phone works now."

"Call? Oh yes," she said walking backward down the hall to get to her next class. "I'll call. And thanks."

Permission to return to Kendallwood. She practically danced into English class.

Chapter Sixteen

M arcy and Audrey made their way down the school bus aisle passing seats full of giggling girls to a rear seat. The pep club girls and the cheerleaders were already sounding out cheers and the bus hadn't even pulled out of the Andonburg High School parking lot.

Ridgely had never been much of a threat to Andonburg in previous seasons, so now with Spence on the starting lineup, tonight's game would be a cinch. Being undefeated was a terrific feeling, Marcy thought as she slid into a seat and made room for her friend. Even this early in the season, Andonburg was being much talked about in their league.

Marcy studied the mauve sunset as they drove west out of Andonburg, out of their familiar hilly country toward the flatter Oklahoma prairie land toward Ridgely.

"Why so mum?" Audrey asked. "Saving your breath for the game?"

The girls had been singing victory songs, but now there was a lull. "Just thinking. Did I tell you that Spence offered to let me use Kendallwood estates again?"

Audrey clutched at her arm. "Marcy how exciting. How did he find out?"

Briefly Marcy told the story about Spence meeting Wesley and the big blowup with Dub Weston. Then she added, "But after thinking it over, I'm not so sure I should accept his invitation."

"Not accept? How crazy is that? All this time it's all you could think about. Your longing to go back and use the grounds just like before."

"That's just it. It's *not* like before. And it never will be."

"Well, if not it's certainly the next best thing. I sure wouldn't throw it aside that easily. Everything can't always be perfect, you know."

Marcy shrugged. "For all I know his family may be totally destroying the wilderness effect. I haven't been there to see."

"And you're telling me that's your only problem? The wilderness effect?"

That was Audrey—always so perceptive. "It's Cissy," she answered lowering her voice even more. They were already whispering so no one would hear the mention of the name of Spence Caldwell.

"I thought so."

"You and I both know she would flip out if she knew I was going up there now that Spence lives there. Her heart is set on him. More so than I've ever seen her with any guy. It's unreal."

Audrey leaned closer and whispered. "It's your life, Marcy. Just go on up there and don't tell her. Because if you don't, you'll always wish you had." Then she added, "You like him too, don't you."

Marcy couldn't answer. She just nodded. Audrey patted her like a mother. Audrey always understood.

The game went well at first. The Andonburg fans, led by the pep club, pep band, and cheerleaders were wild with excitement and enthusiasm. Then Spence began to get clobbered. It wasn't until Dub and Carson were benched that Marcy learned what had happened. They'd been leaving Spence wide open refusing to block for him.

Marcy was incredulous. Didn't they care about the team? About the title of being undefeated? Spence was good, but no one can win a game single-handedly. The game was lost by one point.

"It was because Coach benched Dub and Carson that we lost the lousy thing," said a voice near Marcy's elbow as they pushed through the crowd toward the waiting bus.

"Yeah," agreed a second voice, "he should have known they was just having a little fun. After all, they been our heroes all these years."

Still another voice chimed in the grousing. "If that Caldwell is going to cause our guys to get kicked out of the game, maybe we're better off without him. At least last year we beat Ridgely."

Marcy clinched her fists. She wanted to scream at them to shut up. How dare they put the blame on Spence?

"Poor Spence," Audrey said as they made their way to the waiting bus.

Marcy wondered how many other students felt the same way. After all, Dub and Carson were the *hometown heroes.* In the eyes of many, they could do no wrong.

If she had had doubts before, she was sure now. First thing in the morning she would call Spence and set up a time to come up to Kendallwood, no matter what Cissy said or thought. If it hadn't been for Cissy causing Dub to get mad at Spence, none of this mess would have happened.

Ridgely was one of the worst teams in the league and they won. Marcy's thoughts went to Spence now riding home on the players' bus. It must be awful!

Early Saturday morning, Marcy joined her parents in the kitchen before Cissy woke up. As she had thought, both were pleased to hear of her chance to get back to her work at Kendallwood and were eager to allow her to go.

"We can get your hours adjusted next week," her father said over his coffee mug. "No problem." After blowing and sipping a few times on the hot coffee, he added, "Does Cissy know?"

She winced. "Not yet. Would you not tell her?"

Her mother had been busy at the stove cooking up a batch of scrambled eggs. Now she turned to look at Marcy. "Is that wise? Where are we supposed to tell her you've gone?"

"Tell her I've found a new place."

"Marcy." Her mother's voice was firm.

"Sorry. I guess we'll have to tell her the truth sooner or later." Marcy shook her head wondering what kind of trouble Cissy would give her when she found out. "Maybe Spence won't even be home," she said heading toward the phone.

But he was home, and her heart went wild when his voice came on the line. "Come on up and make yourself at home," he said. "Want me to come get you in the Vette?"

"Oh, uh. No. I mean, no thank you. I was looking forward to the walk."

That was *all* she needed was for him to come sailing up to the house to pick her up. That would crush Cissy for good. Marcy never wanted that. Never in a million years.

17

Chapter Seventeen

The October morning was mellow and golden. The walk up the winding, hilly road, flanked by shady oaks in various hues of yellow and crimson, was exactly what Marcy needed. She walked close to the edge of the road so she could hear the crunch of dry leaves beneath her feet. Her parents agreed that Bitsy should be left behind on this venture.

Reaching the front portico, she moved her nets to her other hand and rang the bell. When Spence opened the door, Marcy gasped. He wore a bandage above his left eye and his chin was cut. When he stepped back to let her in, she noticed he limped slightly.

"Welcome back to Kendallwood, Marcy. Come on in." He looked around then added. "What? No guard dog?"

She laughed at their shared joke. "You're safe. No guard dog today."

She gazed around at the entryway. For so long she'd wanted to stand right here and see the interior of this grand old house. And now she was here. After a moment she turned to him. "Are you all right?"

"I've been better." He grinned. "But I have also been worse. It all evens out."

"Well this looks more worse than better if you ask me."

He politely laughed at her lame joke. But she realized she did come to chat. "I don't want to take your time. I need to get to work. The state fair comes up in a couple of weeks." She shook her nets to emphasize her point.

"And I want to let you get to work, but Aunt Daisy would have a fit if I didn't bring you back to say hello." He took the nets from her. "I'll take these. Follow me."

She followed him through the expanse of the room past draped furniture and in and out around tools, table saws, boards, stacks of ceiling tiles and other paraphernalia needed for remodeling. There appeared to be no defacement of the original flooring or woodwork. For that Marcy was thankful.

In a cozy breakfast nook off the kitchen, Daisy Vandyne stood precariously on a utility stool hanging ruffled pale green curtains. As they approached, she turned to give Marcy a warm smile. "Just a minute," she told them. "Almost finished." Once the curtain rod was firmly in place she descended and came over to Marcy with an outstretched hand.

"Well now. We meet again, Marcy. Welcome." She took Marcy's hand and held it for a moment. "And Spence tells me that you're interested in the study of insects."

"Yes ma'am. I am."

"That's wonderful, my dear. That means you have an inquisitive mind. That's a good sign you know."

Marcy didn't know. She's been told her mind was stale and dull.

"We want you to know," Aunt Daisy continued, "that you're welcome to come here anytime. I realize winter is right around the corner and you can't do much with your insects then, but now, and again in the spring, come as much as you like. We want you to enjoy the place just as you did before we arrived."

Marcy felt lightheaded. Surely, she must be dreaming. It would be impossible to express what this meant to her. She simply offered her thanks and then added, "I'll try not to get in anyone's way."

"Too much land around here to get in anyone's way." The voice from behind her was Uncle Fred who'd just come into the kitchen.

"And that's the truth," Spence added. "About thirty acres or so. Come on now. Time's a-wasting."

He led her through the back halls, past other rooms leading off the halls, finally to a back door that opened onto a spacious covered porch that was walled up about waist-high. At times, she'd come up to this porch to survey the grounds from this vantage point. Now that she looked it over once again, she could see that someone had been clearing out underbrush, but not extensively. A new addition was a greenhouse off to the side of the stone patio. As she breathed in the sharp fall air, she could feel Spence watching her.

"Well? What do you think?"

"Think?" She was puzzled. Why should he give a flip what she thought of the place? "It's fine. Just fine."

"Were you worried we'd ruin it?"

Now she blushed. How could he have known? "Sort of."

"Pennington told me you really liked being up here. Said the place had a special meaning for you."

How could Wesley have told him so much in so short a time? She'd never thought of boys talking of such things. She thought all they knew to talk about was football, horses, and Saturday nights.

"I did spend a lot of time here." She sat down on the rock wall. "It grows on you."

"I agree." He turned to look across the rolling tree-studded hills. "We're working to locate the original walkways and re-lay the stones for the formal garden areas. Then we plan to cultivate the wild grasses and flowers out from that in a type of wilderness garden."

Marcy looked up at him. He was standing close with his hand very near her arm. The soft fall sunshine lent a glow to his hair and caused his blue eyes to squint. His dimples appeared like magic whenever he smiled at her. "A wilderness garden?" Only last evening she'd expressed to Audrey her fear of losing the *wilderness* effect.

"Sound crazy?"

"Sounds wonderful. The wild tangle is the special part I love the most."

"You're not much like your sister, are you?"

She gave a nervous laugh and felt the magical moment sprint away on crystal wings. "No. I'm afraid not." All her life she'd been compared to Cissy.

"C'mon," he said. "I'll show you the greenhouse then let you get on with your work." He picked up her nets.

Hopping down off the wall she followed him down the stone steps. "Let's go." She forced a tone of cheerfulness back into her voice.

The greenhouse was a warm, fragrant respite from the chilly wind. Shelves and tables were full of blooming specimens, some of which Marcy recognized, many she did not.

"Uncle Fred is a whiz with plants." Spence closed the door behind them. "He talks to them like they were people. He has a special touch."

Marcy walked dreamily through the rows of colorful carnations, roses, and forced-blooming tulips. It brought to mind the floral displays that were near the entomology exhibits at the fair.

She turned to look at Spence. "The night of the fair. You were looking at the floral exhibits. That's why you were there, right?"

Now he seemed to be uncomfortable which made her wish she'd said nothing. "You're right. I, uh, I like to check out new exhibits to share with Uncle Fred."

She had no idea what made him stammer, but quickly changed the subject. "I think it was despicable for Dub and Carson to give you such a hard time at the game the other night. And I agree with Coach for taking them out of the game. I bet you're having second thoughts about small-town life."

"Thank for your vote of confidence, but I'm not sure if the situation were reversed if I wouldn't feel the same way. It's difficult for them to have me coming in hogging in on their territory."

"Their territory? My goodness. They don't own Andonburg. There's plenty of room for another football player." His leniency exasperated her.

"Possibly. That is, if it were just another player. But not an all-star champion whose father dares to come to the game in a black limo."

She was surprised at his reference to his father. She would never have mentioned it, but he seemed to want to bring it up. "I see what you mean. I guess it is a bit much for a rancher boy like Dub to swallow."

Reaching out to touch an apricot-colored rose, she added, "My father moved down here from Chicago twenty years ago. He is still looked upon as an outsider. You're lucky you're a descendent of the Kendallwoods or the town folk would be even more distant."

"I've thought of that. A small blessing in disguise I suppose. Still, it can get pretty uncomfortable in the locker room."

"I'm sorry."

"It's not your fault."

"I know. But Dub..."

"Dub's not so bad. I've met his kind before."

That was difficult for Marcy to imagine. She thought Dub was a one-of-a-kind mess.

She started for the door. "I'll get to work now. Thanks for showing me the greenhouse. I love it."

He stepped over and opened the door for her.

Grabbing her nets and adjusting her backpack she headed off toward the pond.

Chapter Eighteen

Her search was a success, turning up several valuable specimens. Three large chrysalises which she would have to research to identify. Also, several clusters of insect eggs beneath the leaves, a dragonfly, plus four beetles. Best of all, that was the day she caught her coveted tiger beetle.

She emerged from the gardens toward the front of the house and was headed down the driveway when Spence called out.

"Hey, Marcy. Aunt Daisy wants to know if you will stay for sandwiches."

The sound of him saying her name sent her heart pounding. Again.

"I'd like to, but I have to be at work soon."

He laughed. "Back to the salt mines, huh?"

"Something like that."

"Well the least I can do is give you a ride home."

She started to protest, but now he was insistent. "It's one thing for you to walk out here, but now you have to get to work. It'll only take a few minutes. I'll be back before Aunt Daisy can get the peanut butter on my sandwich. What would she say if I let you walk all the way home?"

"I've done it many times. Even in the summer heat."

"I know but I wasn't here to offer!"

"That's right. You weren't," she said softly.

Somehow he managed to maneuver the nets into the small car, and after he ran in to tell Aunt Daisy he was off on a mission, Marcy was sitting beside him in the low-slung car feeling as though someone had made a huge mistake. Surely someone would stop them and tell her to get out. That she did not belong in that spot.

"Did you have much luck this morning?" Spence asked as the Vette came down out of the hills and into the edge of town.

"Some beetles and several chrysalises. I finally got a dragonfly, but I think I ruined one of the wings." She kept her answers general.

"What direction will you take with all that?" he asked.

"Direction? Well, the beetles and butterflies are for my general case that I've been building up for a couple of years. The dragonfly will go into the aquatic collection." Even as she explained she wondered what difference it could possibly make to him.

"You've already got a good variety of beetles and butterflies, don't you? Isn't that a little humdrum? Why not take a different bent to your research?"

Was he making fun of her? What could he possibly know about her projects?

"Home or store?" he asked as they approached the bottom of the hill.

"Home." She would have to change clothes before going to work. Then she said, "I never look at any insects as humdrum. All are interesting to me." It sounded defensive she knew, but it was an automatic reaction when it came to her work.

"I just meant that it's what everyone else does. Did you ever think of doing a full display on harmful insects? Not as pretty as butterflies, but attention getting."

Marcy's voice was cool now. "I think I'm doing fine, thank you. I've been studying, researching, and collecting for four years now. I ought to know if I'm going in the right direction."

The big football player was turning out to be like everyone else—critical of her work. She had no time to think further on the dead-end conversation for as they pulled up out front Cissy came running out of the house. She sprinted around to the driver's side talking gaily to Spence as though he drove up in his Corvette every day of the week.

"Oh Spence. Your eye," she cooed, reaching out to touch the bandage. "How perfectly dreadful. That Dub ought to be tarred and feathered for being so hateful. Say, Spence," she went on with hardly a breath in between, "my folks called and need me at the store right away. You wouldn't want to give me a lift, would you? I mean, I wouldn't want to bother you, but since you're right here and all…"

"Sure, Cissy." Spence flashed his dimples in a wide smile. "Be glad to. Hop in."

Cissy looked across the top of the car at Marcy who was standing on the curb with her back pack and nets. Cissy glanced heavenward and mouthed, "Thank goodness."

"Marcy," Cissy said in her motherly tone as she came around to get in, "your lunch is on the table and mother said for you to come on down as quick as you can. See you later."

"I always come as quick as I can without you telling me," Marcy muttered to herself as the red car sped down the shade-dappled street. Suddenly, she hated herself, all the insects, the nets, her work, her displays, and the whole world in general. Why had she gotten so defensive with Spence just when she was getting to know him?

She stepped inside to be greeted by a tail-wagging Bitsy. Nice that at least one member of the family was home at mid-day. "Oh Bitsy," she said leaning down to rub a silky ear, "what's the use? No matter how I try, I always botch it."

Chapter Nineteen

B y the night of the next game, which was a home game, Coach York had devised major changes in the lineup and in the plays for Andonburg High to ensure Spence's safety. The team had lost their undefeated title, but Coach seemed determined that the team would not go completely down the tubes. Dub and Carson were on the bench a good deal. The Andonburg Antelopes had charged ahead by six points and the crowd was exuberant.

Marcy was breathless from all the cheering and her legs felt like two icicles. Even her lungs felt frozen as she yelled each cheer. At half time she was thankful for the cup of hot chocolate Audrey had waiting for her. They huddled on the bleachers together to talk.

"The limousine's here again." Audrey's usually pale cheeks were pink from the cold wind and her voice held a tremor of excitement. "This time there are two men with him rather than only one. And I know why they're here."

Marcy gazed at her friend. For Audrey to get this excited was rare. "Okay, smart girl. Who are they?"

"Football scouts from the university."

Marcy was quiet for a moment. "Of course! College scouts. They *would* be on his trail." She scalded her lips as she sipped the foamy liquid. "What else do you know?"

"What I do know, I don't understand." She glanced around to guarantee secrecy. "It seems as though they are chasing Spence and he's running away."

Marcy let these words soak in. "Perhaps that partly explains why he's come to Andonburg in the first place," she said half to herself.

Then Audrey poked her in the ribs. "Look."

There the forceful Mr. Caldwell, looking like a bear in his long overcoat, had Spence cornered at the edge of the field, talking to him in low tones. No one in the stadium could have missed the scene that was being played out. Marcy sensed that the younger Caldwell was extremely ill at ease in his father's presence.

The game was in the third quarter when Marcy decided she must get her furry earmuffs from the car. Otherwise, her numb ears were going to break and fall off. Cissy scolded her for being such a pansy. "None of the rest of us needs ear muffs. What will you do when it *really* gets cold?"

"Wear my ear muffs," she called back as she headed for the car. It was parked in the next to the last row of the parking lot. As she crawled in to look for the ear muffs, she heard a harsh voice near the back of the car.

"I don't know what's gotten into that kid. He's gone completely insane. Wants to throw years of tradition down the drain. Totally ungrateful for the years his grandfather and I built the name of Caldwell into the annals of the University. We paved the way for him. Gave him everything he would ever want and he thumbs his nose at all of it."

Out the rear window, she saw Mr. Caldwell pacing beside his car that gleamed beneath the stadium lights like a funeral hearse. His two companions leaned against the car listening to his rant.

"Can't you change his mind, Caldwell?" one of the men offered. "Surely he'd listen if he knew what we're offering. Have you explained it in detail?"

"Can you talk to a brick wall? He's just like his mother. Won't listen to good sense." Mr. Caldwell stopped pacing. "There are other ways of convincing someone other than with talk."

Car doors slammed and the motor roared as dust billowed in the graveled drive that led from the athletic field.

So, Spence Caldwell had a tradition to uphold. Probably brought up surrounded by dusty trophies and bronzed cleats used for paperweights. She adjusted the soft muffs on her grateful ears and hurried back to the game.

⋅⁺⋅ ° ♡ °⋅⁺⋅

It was a surprise to the junior class when Maureen called a class meeting in late October. Their class president happened to be in Missouri for a family funeral, so Maureen as vice president obtained permission from Mr. Boley, the principal, to hold a special, unscheduled meeting.

"Mr. Boley is no different than anyone else in Andonburg," Audrey proclaimed to Marcy over lunch in the noisy cafeteria. "He's helplessly vulnerable to Maureen's aura and charm." She put a finger under her chin and attempt a coy expression which made Marcy chuckle.

"She does have a way about her," Marcy agreed, remembering the incident with the cheerleader's blouses and other matters in which Maureen had repeatedly gotten her own way.

But at least she didn't have to live with Maureen Ratherfield. She did have to live with Cissy Hankins, and after her little ride in the Corvette last Saturday, the girl was impossible.

Marcy didn't dare mention her time of talking privately with Spence in the greenhouse and on the back patio. Not that it mattered. She was sure now that Spence was simply being polite. But she had to admit his attitude was a far cry from the ridicule to which she had become accustomed.

"What do you think the meeting's about?" Audrey asked as they cleared their table to leave.

Marcy shrugged. "Who knows? But you can bet it'll be for Maureen's benefit in some way."

They deposited their trays on the conveyer and hurried to the library where the *emergency* meeting was being held during the lunch hour. Marcy was wondering what had happened to her to cause her to all of a sudden be so cynical? Things seemed backward. She used to scold others for making fun of Maureen.

As it turned out Maureen presented a plan for a dance. A Fall Festival, as she called it. Not such a bad idea, Marcy reasoned as she watched Maureen handling the crowd of classmates.

"It'll be a fun way to raise money," Maureen was saying in her slow drawl. "We'll make the rule that all class members can invite someone from another class level or from another school, but it will still be our class party. We'll have a cover charge and sell refreshments." With a wave of her hand, she added, "It seems to me anything we can do to raise funds for our senior trip next year is important. And this will be no work at all."

"No work?" someone protested. "Who will print up and sell the tickets?"

"And put together the refreshments?" added another.

"And decorations?" came yet another.

Maureen laughed her delicate laugh. "Oh, you know what I mean. That isn't work. It's just plain old fun."

Before they knew it, the Andonburg junior class had voted in the Fall Festival and started appointing various *work* committees. But, of course, it wasn't *work*.

Marcy refused to take part. She knew she wouldn't be going to the dance and she didn't need yet another drain on her time.

Later in the afternoon between classes, Cissy rushed up to her and Audrey in the hallway. "Marcy, I've got to talk to you. Sorry Audrey." She waved her hand to shoo her away. "But this is top secret. Personal. All that stuff."

"Now see here, Cissy," Marcy protested.

"No problem," Audrey said calmly. "I've got to get to class anyway. See you."

"Cissy, that was beyond rude. What's gotten into you?" Marcy struggled to hold her anger as she watched her friend walk away.

"I'm sorry, Marcy, but I had to talk to you. I need your help desperately. Desperately!"

Marcy let out a sigh. "What now?"

"Marcy, why do you think Maureen came up with the idea of a class party?"

"She already told us. It's to raise money for the class." Then Marcy recalled what she herself had said earlier about it being for Maureen's benefit.

"No, silly. It's because of Spence."

"Spence? What's he got to do with this?"

"She planned it so she could be the one to ask him to the dance. She purposely set up a class dance with the rule that we could ask those from another grade level. Now she's plotting how she can ask him this very afternoon."

Marcy didn't want to hear another word. And she for sure didn't want to know how her sister had learned all this scuttlebutt. It was all so ridiculous. "We'll talk about it after school. It's late. I don't want to have to report to the office for a tardy slip."

Cissy grabbed her arm. "Not after school. That'll be too late."

Marcy broke free and was walking backward down the hall. "After next class then." Quickly she turned and hurried away. Why oh why did her sister's life have to be so melodramatic?

Chapter Twenty

M arcy hoped against hope that she could evade Cissy for the rest of the afternoon, but it was an impossible task. She was discovered in the girls' restroom.

"There you are!" Cissy gushed as she entered. "Come where we can talk quietly." Then proceeded to practically drag Marcy to the far side of the school library next to the windows. "Now," she said matter-of-factly, "help me think of a way to get Spence away before Maureen can ask him to the dance."

"How can you be so sure she even wants to ask him?"

Cissy rolled her eyes. "I'm not blind. She's been after him since day one. What can I do, Marcy? You're the brainy one in the family."

Marcy cringed and turned to gaze out the window to the school yard so Cissy wouldn't notice her expression. If she were so smart she'd be asking him herself. But that probably never occurred to her twin.

Suddenly she desperately wanted to get away. Noticing the younger kids playing a game of touch football, she said, "Why not have Bernie and his buddies kidnap Spence. They love him too you know."

"Of course. Marcy, that's it. Sure, the younger guys love him. They can corral him and divert him from Maureen's path. It's a wonderful idea." She gave Marcy a quick hug. "How can I ever thank you?"

"I'll think of something," she mumbled.

"But if Bernie knows it's for me, he'll balk."

"Bribe him."

"With what?"

"With jobs. Offer to do his work."

"Ugh. Do you realize what some of his jobs are? Picking up dog poop in the yard; taking out the garbage. Gross."

Marcy shrugged. "How bad to you want it?"

"Bad, Marcy. Bad." She paused. "Would you help me pay it off?"

Marcy could hardly believe what she was hearing. Was there no end to the gall of this girl? "This is your show, not mine."

"Okay, okay. Can't hurt to ask. At least you can go find Bernie and tell him the plan. He can ask Spence to come to our house and teach him and the other guys some of the plays. As soon as we're off work we can walk home. He'll be there and I can ask him to the dance." Her eyes grew wide. "Oh Marcy, do you think it'll work?"

Marcy turned away. "The bell, Cissy. See you after school."

It wasn't easy locating Bernie when the time came. She had to track him down and get him to the high school parking lot where he would intercept Spence while Cissy kept an eye out for Maureen.

Bernie thought it was a great plan. Win-win for him. Time with Spence and his chores done by Cissy for three whole days.

By the time Bernie and Marcy reached the place where Cissy was waiting, Cissy was frantic. Spence was walking out across the parking lot to the Corvette and suddenly Maureen came out of the school building from another direction. Like a shot, Bernie ran interference and cut her off. The twins watched the drama from a safe distance.

Before they knew it, Spence was nodding and pointing to the car door inviting Bernie to hop in. Maureen paused for a bit, then turned to walk to her own car.

˖⁺·₊ ° ♡ °₊·⁺˖

As they walked to the drug store, and during their after-school work hours, Cissy could not let up. "Do you suppose she followed him? What if she's already asked him? What if he's not even there when we get there? Maybe he has to get home. Oh, Marcy, how can I bear this not knowing?"

Marcy wondered how she could bear the drivel. "You can bear it, Cissy. Just keep busy and occupy your mind." In desperation she asked her father if they could change out the window display. The work didn't stop Cissy's fretting, but it did slow it down some.

"Marcy," Cissy said as they walked to the house later, "if I get this date, I'll never stop thanking you. You and Bernie both have been so great. I don't know what I'd do without you."

She should have been sensitive to the compliment, since Cissy didn't give out many, but she had no heart to hear anything her sister had to say. She didn't even reply.

˖⁺·₊ ° ♡ °₊·⁺˖

They heard the shouts coming from their back yard before they ever reached the house. Cissy quickened her steps. As they rounded the side of the house there was Spence surrounded by a pack of young football hopefuls. Spence was quite obviously enjoying himself. Marcy noticed how patient he was with each of the kids. She didn't know another guy in Andonburg who would have done such a thing.

He looked their way as they entered the shrubbery-lined yard.

"Oh Spence," Cissy said, "it's so nice to have you at our house again. I bet you're thirsty. Marcy, why don't you go get everyone something to drink?"

By the time Marcy had put together an ample supply of iced punch and brought it out on a tray with a large stack of paper cups, she knew beyond a doubt that Cissy had asked Spence to the dance, and Spence had said yes.

Even though she had known all day it would turn out that way, she couldn't control the wrenching pain inside. She placed the tray on the picnic table and turned to go back in.

"Marcy," Spence called out.

She stopped, full of fear that tears might come. Cissy must never know.

"You're coming, too, right?"

"Coming?"

"To the Fall Festival." He was beside her now.

She cleared her throat. "I don't think so, Spence. That gives me a free evening. I can't remember ever being this behind in my work."

"I thought sure you'd ask that Pennington fellow. Hoped we could make it a foursome again. He's a nice guy."

"Wesley *is* a nice guy," she said too quickly, almost defensively. Then she realized that Spence truly meant it. He really did think that Wesley was an okay guy. How different. "No, I'm not asking anyone. As I said, I'm using the time to get caught up." She turned and went inside.

Chapter Twenty-One

Trusty 4-H leader, Mrs. O'Bannon, offered to take all club members' exhibits to the Tulsa State Fair on opening day. Marcy hated to release her things into the hands of the hefty lady and her two wild little boys. Her cases were fragile. But there was no way she could get away to take them herself, and no one else would be going the day before the fair opened. Besides, Mrs. O'Bannon knew the ins and outs of getting exhibits correctly registered.

"Are your exhibits entered?" Spence asked her before class the next day.

She was so surprised that he remembered. "Delivered by Mrs. O'Bannon, our club leader," she told him. "At least I think she made it there safely with everything."

"When will you know the results?"

"Cissy and I will drive over Saturday, stay the night and come back Sunday." Then she added, "Our aunt lives in Tulsa. We'll stay at her house."

Marcy had wanted to make the trip alone, but her parents would never agree to that. Cissy would have to go along. That meant Marcy would have to take in the noisy midway.

"The suspense is maddening, isn't it."

"Always." Was she dreaming? It was as though he identified with her intense desire to win.

"You'll do okay," he assured her as they walked into the classroom.

Even with humdrum butterflies? she wanted to ask. But she was determined not to botch it this time. She smiled a thank you and went to take her seat.

⋆⁺˙⁺˚ ♡ ˚⁺˙⁺⋆

It was early Saturday afternoon when the twins arrived at the fairgrounds. Cissy pulled into the already crowded parking lot behind the long rows of livestock barns. The barnyard aromas filled the air as they locked the car and discussed plans of where and when to meet.

"I assume you want to go to the 4-H building alone as usual," Cissy said fishing in her purse for lip gloss.

"We both know how you hate tears," Marcy remarked. But she wouldn't really cry. Would she?

"Sounds like a negative attitude to me."

"Just bracing myself. Why not meet at the sky-lift in about an hour?"

"An hour?" She applied the gloss and dropped it back into her purse. "That ties me down. I'll be busy looking for Andonburg kids. What if I find some of them and don't make it back there on time?"

"Bring them with you, silly."

"If it's Spence, I'll be glad to oblige." Cissy rolled her eyes. "Seriously though, I so hope he's here. I would be so neat to ride some of the rides with him again."

"And have him bullied by Dub again..." Marcy put in.

The quick retort she expected didn't come. Cissy shifted her purse strap up on her shoulder and thought a moment. "Dub has sort of backed off. He's been quiet lately. Pouting over his discipline from Coach York maybe. I don't know."

"Thank goodness for small miracles."

"Yeah. Thank goodness."

"See you," Marcy said as their paths parted.

Her stomach was churning as she walked past the city of travel trailers belonging to the carnival people, on toward the 4-H building. The pavement was strewn with litter and all the mingling food aromas didn't help her queasy stomach one bit.

At the door of the building she asked a bystander for the location of the entomology exhibits. Slowly she made her way in that direction. She rubbed damp palms against her pants legs. Was it worth all this stress and tension? What if there was a white ribbon hanging from her case? She'd never be able to handle it. She knew she would absolutely sit right down on the cold concrete floor and bawl her head off. If only she'd had more time to do a superb job rather than a half-way job. But still, even Wesley has said her cases were good.

Her eyes scanned the rows of entomology cases, searching for her own. Her heart stopped. There it was—her general-class case—a red. A red! Only a red. The one she'd been building for years. Now fear rose in her throat as she frantically searched for the aquatic collection. Would it be white?

Exasperation set in as she scanned every case and hers was nowhere to be found. Slow down, her brain told her speeding heart. It's got to be here. If anything had happened to it, Mrs. O'Bannon would have called her.

She looked over them one more time. The competition was intense and the cases were plentiful. Then she saw it. The case was in a special display on a tilted stand so all fair-goers could observe. From it fluttered the lavender-colored, Reserve Champion ribbon.

By now she was so pent up she thought surely she would faint, scream, or cry. All she could do was stand and stare. Adjacent to hers, on the same stand was Wesley's moth collection sporting the dark purple Grand Champion ribbon.

"It's all right," she said softly. "It's all right. I don't feel beat out this time. I feel wonderful."

Later that evening, when she got to her aunt's house, she would call home and share her news with her parents. Cissy would act pleased, but Marcy knew she cared nothing about the victory one way or the other.

Eventually, her breathing and pulse rate returned to normal. She wished she'd brought her camera to record the momentous event. As she walked away, she paused to look back at the unbelievable spectacle. She still had time before meeting Cissy and she wanted to savor this moment.

Finally, leaving the entomology area she ambled slowly through the rows upon rows of floral exhibits. It made her think of Uncle Fred's greenhouse.

In the midst of the displays, setting high on a slender white pedestal was a striking arrangement of roses and wild flowers interspersed with native grasses. It was a rare combination. Like denim and lace. Like wild and tame. The tell-tale purple ribbon hung from it.

When she thought of it later, she couldn't explain why she stood and gazed at it for so long. Possibly because of its profound beauty. Stepping closer she read the identification tag on the display. "*Caldwell, Spence.*"

She gasped. "Vandyne, Fred," it should have said. Fred, not Spence. Hadn't Spence said, "Uncle Fred is a whiz with plants?"

Then she remembered his remark to her about the suspense being maddening. No wonder he could relate. It was because he *knew* about the suspense. He knew firsthand!

Marcy had to hurry to go meet Cissy, but all she wanted to do was stand and stare. How much of the greenhouse was Spence's rather than Fred's? How had he learned to do such magnificent things with plants? Perhaps she would never know.

By early evening, the girls were once again with Spence and Wesley. It seems they had purposely met in the parking lot by a pre-arranged plan and then came looking for them. The time together was as painful for Marcy as the evening at the County Fair.

Once when the twins were alone, Cissy grabbed her arm. "Now's the time, Marcy. Now ask Wesley to the dance. Don't pass up this chance. I know he likes you. We'd have so much fun together."

"No, Cissy. It's my decision. Now lay off."

"But you two make such a cute couple. Both crazy about creepy bugs."

Marcy wanted to cry.

Chapter Twenty-Two

Winning the Reserve Champion prize, while exciting, also proved to be sobering. Marcy began to realize that such wins could increase her chances for an academic college scholarship. The fair commission had informed her that her win qualified her to attend a study seminar with the entomology department at State College during spring break.

Now, in addition to cheerleading practice, working at the store, and working on her entomology, she now determined she would spend more time with her studies.

But even in her busiest moments, she continually wondered about Spence's floral exhibit. In the back of her mind, she planned to call again Saturday to ask if she could again visit Kendallwood, that is, if she could finish all her homework in time.

"Sure," Spence said, when she called him the following Saturday. "Come on up. It's a quiet day, and I finished my research report for anatomy class."

"I finished mine as well," she answered brightly, pleased to have something in common with him. She set a time to arrive and shivered as she hung up the phone.

This time, the late-sleeper was up and about. Cissy came into the kitchen all bleary-eyed. "Going to Kendallwood this morning?" she wanted to know.

Marcy nodded, wondering what was next.

"I think I'll come along this time. I've been wanting to see how they've remodeled the old place. I never thought anything could be done with it."

Marcy froze. All the magic would disappear if Cissy tagged along. "They're *restoring* the house, Cissy," she said. "Not remodeling."

"Whatever. Anyway, I want to see it."

Mercifully, their father laid aside his newspaper he'd been reading while eating his breakfast. "Cissy," he said calmly, but in a matter-of-fact tone, "you were never interested enough to accompany Marcy when no one lived there. I think this is Marcy's thing and she should go alone as usual. Besides, we need you at the store in an hour. I'll let you off early this afternoon."

Marcy dared not even glance at Cissy.

Her father then added, "It's a little nippy outside. You can drop us off at the store then take the car up there today."

"Thanks so much," she said as she rounded the table to give him a big hug. Cissy gave her a sour look.

⁺⋅₊ ° ♡ ° ₊⋅⁺

"Hey," Spence said, answering her knock and looking out to notice the car. "You're not hoofing it this time. Terrific."

He ushered her into the entryway, where she had to stop a moment and stare. New plush carpet graced the sweeping stairway, above which hung a splendid gold and crystal chandelier. Inlaid oak flooring beneath their feet held a pale golden glow. She never imagined the place could be so beautiful now that loving touches had been added.

"Better?" he asked.

"Much more than better." She wasn't even embarrassed at having stared. To see the ongoing restoration process was like a dream come true for her.

Hellos were exchanged with Aunt Daisy and Uncle Fred who were busy with tile flooring in the sun room. From there Spence led her out the back door where they were greeted with a sharp, cold wind.

"Where will you find insects today?" Spence asked, zipping up his jacket.

"Under rocks and old logs. It's amazing what I can find."

"Smart girl." He pointed to the greenhouse. "Want to see our latest beauties before you start work?"

"Indeed I do, Grand Champion winner."

He had taken her arm as they descended the steps and at her words, he stopped and turned to face her. She was a step above him and his face was close. He smiled. She stopped breathing.

"The observant entomologist misses nothing."

"How could a person miss such an entry I'd like to know? Sitting on a pedestal, looking breathtakingly lovely beyond all imagination."

"Why Marcy Hankins. What a compliment." With that, he closed the gap between them and planted a light kiss on the tip of her nose.

"And why did you say the work here was all Uncle Fred's?"

"And why did you not tell me what you were doing up here the day we first met? Or what you were doing in the back room of the drug store the night I came to get the prescription filled?"

Now she laughed out loud. "Touché."

"Sounds like we have similar dilemmas."

"Sounds like it."

He took her arm again and led her across the stone patio to the greenhouse, opened the door, and ushered her inside. "Were you surprised when you saw it?"

"Shocked is a better word."

"But you haven't told anyone?"

"That's your privilege. It wouldn't be fair to take that away from you."

He gave a grand wave of his hand. "Yes, Marcy, I'll tell the truth now. This is all mine. I've been involved in botany for years. Uncle Fred dabbles in it some and they both love growing things. When they were planning to move here, they invited me to come and help improve the grounds."

Marcy smile. A botanist. Who in Andonburg would believe it?

"They also," Spence went on, "wanted to remove me from the excessive pressures of my father, whose acts you have observed. No doubt with some amusement."

"Oh no, I never..."

"Most people do though. They either laugh at him or they're afraid of him. I imagine most of the old timers around here saw his antics as very funny. The truth is he is *very* influential in business, in politics, and at his alma mater which he desperately wants me to attend. To follow in his footsteps and in his glory."

"And your grandfather's?"

He gave her a puzzled look. "And you knew that how?"

She explained what she had overheard the night we went to the car to fetch her earmuffs.

"That means you already had it all figured out. Yes, *and* my grandfather as well. They were both football stars at the university in their day."

He had stopped midway down one of the aisles, not really showing her the plants and flowers, but rather seeming to want to talk. And she was willing to listen.

"It's crazy," he said, "I'm a good football player with no passion for the game." He sat down on an upturned crate. He looked up at her. "Too bad I wasn't born skinny like your friend, Wesley." He laughed at his own joke.

"Can't you just say no to your father and stick to it? Let him know your life is your own?"

"Sounds easy, doesn't it? And I have been saying no all along. My moving here was saying no. But my father doesn't know how to take no for an answer. He blames my mother for taking me away from football and involving me in botany."

"How sad."

"Now, of course, he's angry with Uncle Fred and Aunt Daisy for inviting me to live with them. He won't come here and visit, but shows up at the football games with scouts in tow. So embarrassing."

He stood up again and started walking. Marcy followed still listening. "The last time we talked, he threatened to stop supporting me and take away the Vette if I refuse to cooperate. But my goal is to attend State and forget about football completely."

"What will you do if he does withhold support?" she asked.

"He and mother are divorced. While my mother has an established florist shop in Oklahoma City, she can't afford to help me much. Uncle Fred plans to pay me to landscape the grounds here, and I thought I might do some business through the greenhouse here." He turned to her. "What do you think?"

"Dad says a person can do anything he sets his mind to do," she told him, pleased that he asked for her input. "But still, you have some heavy decisions to make. Only you can make them."

Here everyone had thought that Spence Caldwell was a carefree guy who had the world by the tail. Everything handed to him on a silver platter. But he'd been suffering through his own struggles.

"Sorry to be so morbid. Come here, I have something to show you." He took her hand and led her toward the back of the greenhouse. "The mums have bloomed since you were here the last time."

Indeed they had. The plants were heavy with huge golden blooms. Spence reached up on a shelf and took down a pair of pruning shears.

"No Spence," she said. "Don't ruin it."

"Ruin it?" He selected one of the largest blooms and snipped the stem. "How can you ruin a flower..." He placed it in her hand and closed her fingers around it. "...by giving it away? It's my gift to you for your Reserve Champion win."

"But I have nothing to give you for your win."

"You just gave it."

"I did? What was it?"

"Listening without scorning. The few people I've told think I'm nuts for turning down such a lucrative offer as my father is giving. But you understood. That was your gift to me."

She looked down at the exquisite blossom in her hand. It was large enough to be an entire bouquet.

"I need to get to work now." Holding up her flower, she added, "I'll put this in the car for now." She turned to go. "Thank you."

"And thank *you*."

23

Chapter Twenty-Three

Cissy begged to know all about the golden chrysanthemum, but Marcy just said it was from Uncle Fred's greenhouse and let it drop. Still she felt that Cissy looked at her strangely and when she did, Marcy remembered the talk in the greenhouse and couldn't help but blush.

On Monday morning before anatomy class, Marcy was worried that when she saw Spence she wouldn't know what to say to him. She and Audrey were already seated in the classroom before he showed up. He smiled at her briefly before he sat down. She let he breath out slowly. At least he was able to look at her.

She had thought perhaps he would be sorry he confided in her. Sometimes after a person shares a confidence, it turns out that it was a bad decision. Was Spence feeling like that?

She continually reminded herself that she had merely been someone for him to confide in—convenient and available. And understanding. The secret must be kept until he made his final decision of whether or not to accept his father's offer. That might not be until after football season was over. Marcy felt privileged to be the only one to know. Still it was a struggle to see him talking to Cissy later that day in the cafeteria.

The decorating committee for the Fall Festival began on Thursday to transform the gym from the mundane to the sublime. Well, as sublime as a high school gym could get. Hay bales, scarecrows, Indian corn, and sheaves of cornstalks were places in strategic places. Gold and russet streamers added to the effect. The air of festivity that permeated the school made Marcy's heart ache, and she had only herself to blame. It was her choice not to be a part. She knew Wesley would have taken her if she'd only asked. And she could, even at this late date, call him and he would say yes and escort her to the dance. But she was adamant. She refused to ask just so she could go. That would be unfair.

A light skiff of snow fell all through the day on Friday, which was the day of the Fall Festival. Perhaps it should have been a Winter Wonderland dance, Marcy thought to herself as she watched Cissy all in a dither trying to get herself ready to go.

"Maureen drove all the way to Fort Smith last week to buy a new dress for the dance," Cissy moaned, staring at the emerald green dress spread across her bed. Marcy turned a deaf ear. What should it matter to her what Maureen wore when she had Spence to herself for one whole evening?

Hurriedly, Marcy gathered what she needed to go to the store to work for the evening. Thankfully, she was already on her way before Spence arrived.

In her mind she could see the shiny candy-apple red Corvette coming to a stop at the curb and Spence getting out and rising to his full height. He'd be dressed in a grey-blue sports jacket that complimented his blue eyes and light hair. She could even conjure up the memories of the fragrance of his after shave. Then she wondered if he would kiss Cissy good-night?

With a jolt, she shook off the depressing thoughts. The evening held the chill of the snow, clear and still. Muted street lights reflected soft shadows on the layer of fresh snow. She stepped up her pace; she determined she would make the most of the time she had tonight.

Entering her workroom, she set about examining every specimen and double-checking them against the entries in the log book to see where she stood. Once again in her negligence, she'd lost a few good specimens. Later, as she gingerly handled a butterfly on the spreading block, she recalled what Spence had said about an exhibit of harmful insects.

She had pushed the idea aside until just this moment. That's because when it was mentioned she thought he was making fun. Now she knew differently. After seeing his entry in the state fair, she realized he knew what would catch the judge's eye—something unique.

She rose from her worktable and stepped to the window and stared out at the darkened alleyway. Smiling, she remembered the day she and Cissy were painting the desk and Spence walked up. What a sultry day it had been, and now snow covered the ground. Back then, she thought Kendallwood had been taken from her, but it had now been restored to her many times over.

Turning from the window she stood there for a time surveying the worktable. Too big, is what she was thinking. A project like Spence suggested was too big. Self doubt washed over her. "I could never pull it off," she whispered. "Insects I know, but plants I..." There was a catch in her throat. "But plants I don't know. But guess who does? The botanist who lives at Kendallwood, that's who."

Of course. Spence would know each plant that the harmful insects threatened to destroy. Excitement stirred within her. Should she propose such a joint project to him? Perhaps for the spring science fair?

Returning to her worktable, she pulled reference books from off the shelf and began flipping through them making feverish notes on a yellow legal pad. In a flash, she knew she must resign her position as cheerleader. She would do it at the end of football season, before basketball season started.

It had been all wrong for her from the beginning. Who was she to be telling Spence to say *no* and mean it when she hadn't been able to? Once the decision was made about cheerleading, a mental fetter snapped. She was instantly free. The pressure disappeared.

All realization of time was lost as she pored over the books, so when Cissy came barging in at eleven, she was startled.

When she first heard the key in the front door, she had thought her father was coming to fill an emergency prescription as he often did at all hours. But in a moment there was Cissy leaning against the doorframe of the workroom. She flung her coat on a nearby chair. On her wrist was a corsage of small russet mums arranged with wheat heads among them. Marcy had no doubt it was Spence's original creation.

"Home so early?" she asked. "Did you have a good time?" Cissy was quiet, so Marcy asked, "What are you doing here and not at home?"

Still silence. From Cissy, any and all noise was normal. Silence was abnormal. Marcy studied her sister's face. "Something's wrong."

Cissy snorted. "*That's* an understatement."

Marcy's heart filled with compassion. In spite of her sister's shortcomings, she loved her dearly and hated to see her hurt. "Bring up and chair and tell me."

Cissy didn't sit down but chose to pace as she talked, stopping now and then to gaze out the window. "Guess how I went to the dance, Marcy."

"Why, you were with Spence in this Vette."

"Wrong."

"Wrong? He didn't come?"

"Oh, he came all right. In his uncle's *station wagon*."

Her tone made it sound as though he came for her in a garbage truck. Marcy's breath caught. Spence's father had followed through on his threat of taking away the Corvette. That meant Spence had made his decision. But why so soon, she wondered.

"But that was only the beginning of troubles," Cissy went on, pacing again.

Marcy sighed. "What else?"

"Guess what the Andonburg star football player wanted to talk about?"

Talk about. Talk about. What would Spence talk about if he couldn't share about his beloved plants? She couldn't imagine. "Tell me."

"You!"

"Me?"

"You." Bitterness edged her voice. "He wanted to know all about your work here. How it was set up. How long you'd been doing it. You name it, he asked it."

But of course, she thought. Spence had opened up and shared gut-level with her, and yet she'd never even offered to let him see her workroom. How shallow she'd been.

Cissy finally acquiesced to the nearby chair and Marcy reached out and touched her sister's arm. "Cissy, I'm so sorry."

"Usurped by a Bug Brain!" She shook her head. "Unbelievable." Now she looked squarely at Marcy. "You know, I think he likes you. *Really* likes you."

Marcy's entire body was aflame. She pressed fingers to her throat unsure she could even swallow. But Cissy didn't seem to notice. She wasn't finished. "Guess what else?"

Marcy rose to get a glass of water. "I'm fresh out of guesses."

Cissy slouched in the chair and let her hands go limp in her lap. "I was jealous of Maureen being with Dub."

Marcy's voice went soft. "Oh Cissy." She sat back down, took several sips of water and tried to process all she was hearing.

"Ever since he flubbed up the Ridgely game, he's been on his best behavior. After that, when I was madly chasing after Spence, he's never given me a bad time about it. Now I realize I was wishing he would." She looked up with sad puppy eyes. "I guess I like him more than I thought." She managed a slight smile. "All evening, he kept cutting in on Spence and me."

"He's always been crazy about you, Cissy."

She straightened up in her chair. "Hey, those football scouts who came to watch Spence also got an eyeful of Dub's playing as well. Would you believe he stands a chance at a football scholarship?"

All this time, Marcy's forceful, dynamic, determined twin hadn't really known what she wanted after all. Ironic.

"That *is* good news, Cissy. What say we talk home together? Get your coat. Mom and Dad will be wondering where we are."

Marcy doused the lights and the two walked across the darkened store arm in arm.

24

Chapter Twenty-Four

Another layer of soggy clinging snow had fallen and the grounds of Kendallwood estates were transformed into a mystical, frosted, fantasy world. The snow crunched beneath their feet as Spence and Marcy walked hand-in-hand down the hill to the pond.

"Did I wake you with my call?" His voice broke the silence.

"Heavens, no," she answered. "I'm always up before six on Saturdays. Especially in winter." She felt as light as the soft flakes sifting down.

"Hated to call early, but I was anxious to tell you about the decision that I finally made."

"I knew already." Miniature snowballs rolled in front of her boots with each step.

"How?"

"When Cissy announced she rode to the dance in the station wagon."

"Oh yeah. Was she disappointed?"

"Well, riding in a Corvette is a kick."

"Are *you* disappointed?"

"Just being with you for me is a kick." And it was true. When he offered to drive down to get her that morning, she made no protest. She was thrilled to be with him.

He gave her gloved hand a squeeze. "The decision wasn't the only thing I wanted to tell you. I wanted you to know how I came to make it."

"My curiosity is killing me."

"It was because of you."

She slowed her step to look up at his face. To see if he was kidding. She could never be that strong an influence on anyone's life. "Please explain."

"The night of the Ambrose County Fair, when Dub called you a Bug Brain, I realised the pressure and the misunderstanding you lived with because of your work. Most of your friends don't understand you at all."

"True," she agreed, "but not to the point of being stoned."

He laughed. "I know, Marcy, but you're so great about it. I knew I needed to be like that. To have my work known and let the chips fall where they may. So, I told Dad the money made no difference to me. I'll be entering State next fall."

"Was he angry?"

They had walked until they were in a grove of cedars near the water's edge. One had a large branch with a straight, low angle to it. Spence brushed the snow away and easily lifted her to sit on it, and continued.

"I guess angry would be the right word. He wasted no time getting here to take the Vette away." He was quiet for a moment. "Now I know it's time for me to lead my life in the way I feel the most comfortable, and in the way I'm the most productive."

"And I agree. That's why when I was putting notes together for a project on harmful insects, I realized I would have no more time for cheerleading. I'm turning in my resignation at the end of football season."

"Harmful insects?" He brightened. "You *did* consider it? It was rather rude of me to suggest it."

"No, it's a good idea. But I want to display each along with the plants they destroy. Or a sketch. Whichever works." She broke off a twig from the branch and made designs in the snow beside her. "I'll need a lot of help if I'm going to have it ready for the spring science fair."

"Is that an invitation?"

"You're the botanist."

"I accept, Miss Entomologist." He was leaning against the tree still holding her hand. "I care a great deal about you, Marcy. I have from the first moment you came flying out of the shrubbery that day. For a long time, I assumed you were taken by Wesley. It wasn't until you passed up the opportunity to ask him to the dance that I wondered if I'd been mistaken."

The morning haze was beginning to clear and Marcy felt the warmth of the sunshine through her coat. She loosened the bright blue muffler at her throat.

"Hungry?" he asked.

"I am."

"Aunt Daisy's fixing her best homemade doughnuts. And with hot chocolate. Sound good?"

"Sounds wonderful."

He placed his hands on her waist and gently lifted her down from the low-hanging limb. Her feet barely touched the ground before he was holding her very close. "It'll be a large project," he whispered.

"I know," she whispered back. "Probably take simply hours and hours of hard work."

"Together."

"Together," she agreed.

"Here at Kendallwood. In your workroom. In the greenhouse..." He kissed her lips softly between each.

"We'll have to start right away."

Spence's arm remained tightly around her as he led her back up the hill to the house.

Norma Jean Lutz Bio

Norma Jean Lutz's writing career began professionally in 1977 when she enrolled in a writing correspondence course. Since then, she has had over 250 short stories and articles published in both secular and Christian publications. The full-time writer is also the author of over 50 published books under her own name and many ghostwritten books. Her books have been favorably reviewed in *Affair de Coeur, Coffee Time Romance, Romance Reader at Heart, and The Romance Studio* magazines, and her short fiction has garnered a number of first prizes in local writing contests.

Norma Jean is the founder of the Professionalism In Writing School, which was held annually in Tulsa for fourteen years. This writers' conference, which closed its doors in 1996, gave many writers their start in the publishing world.

A gifted teacher, Norma Jean has taught a variety of writing courses at local colleges and community schools, and is a frequent speaker at writers' seminars around the country. For eight years, she taught on staff for the Institute of Children's Literature. She has served as artist-in-residence at grade schools, and for two years taught a staff development workshop for language arts teachers in schools in Northeastern Oklahoma.

As a writer who loves writing for teens, and hanging out with teens, Norma Jean has launched the **Clean Teen Reads** website and blog. Lots of fun stuff for teens! Check it out here:

www.CleanTeenReads.net

The Site for Teens Who Love Books and Stories

Also by

www.ingramcontent.com/pod-product-compliance
Lightning Source LLC
Chambersburg PA
CBHW060441130626

46555CB00005B/2447